AFTER SUNSET

Jim Keane

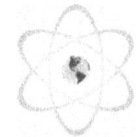

2023, TWB Press
www.twbpress.com

After Sunset
Copyright © 2023 by Jim Keane

Edited by Terry Wright

Cover Art by Terry Wright

ISBN: 978-1-959768-12-8

Chapter One

The rustic hamlet of Montrose, New York, nestled along the Hudson River with its spacious parks, wooded hills, and scenic views, was the last place anyone expected an outbreak to occur, especially on this warm spring evening. The sun had just set as Marty McNamara parked the Mercedes in front of the Save More convenience store, a quick stopover to buy milk and eggs.

Before he could open the car door, his wife Cheryl grabbed his arm. "Wait."

He crooked his eyebrows. "What?"

"How was your workout at the gym today?"

"Good. Why?"

"Who was that floozy you were talking to?"

His heart could have flopped out on the floor mat. "Wha...what?"

"The one wearing the pink outfit that fit her tighter than the noose around your neck right now."

Marty's mouth gaped open. "You were there?"

Cheryl folded her arms. "It looked like you were getting friendly with her."

Marty stabbed an accusatory finger at her. "I can't believe my wife is checking up on me."

"Are you having an affair?"

"Christ, Cheryl, she just works out there. I'm sick of your jealous rants."

"Don't let me see you with her again."

"Then stay away from the gym." He huffed, shoved open the door, and stalked to the store entrance.

"Wait up, Marty."

"I don't need your help buying milk and eggs." He knew it wasn't about shopping, it was about her distrust, her jealous eyes always on the lookout for any woman who might catch his attention, if even for a second. Reluctantly, he opened the door for her. The breeze pushed a torn lottery ticket down the sidewalk. A bell rang above their heads. He smelled hazelnut coffee from a percolator by the front counter.

The clerk, a muscular man in his forties with a

thick beard, took an order from a young couple while a blonde boy and girl stood beside them.

Cheryl squeezed Marty's arm. "I'll get in line to buy us the winning Powerball ticket."

"From your mouth to God's ears. I'm ready for early retirement."

"Pick up some beer to celebrate."

"You got it." He rolled a small shopping cart down the aisle and picked up milk, eggs, and a six-pack of Yonkers IPA then joined Cheryl standing behind the couple with the two kids. "What's up with the clerk?"

"He's got some kind of nervous twitch."

"Looks like he's on something."

"PCP? Meth?"

The clerk's jaw clenched and his nostrils flared. He gripped a can of black beans and crushed it with his bare hand. Beans and juice gushed out. His head kept twisting at weird angles, like his neck was broken, and his face grew mushroom grey. Dark circles formed around his eyes.

The woman waiting with the man and children ushered them backwards toward the door. "What's wrong with you, mister?"

The clerk growled in a guttural tone. "Keep away from me." He hurled the cash register at the woman. It struck her in the face, flooring her, out cold.

"What the hell is your problem?" Her husband lunged at the clerk, grabbed him by the shirt, but the brute tossed the man aside like a bothersome child.

The children screamed and huddled over their downed mother.

Marty and Cheryl stood there in shock, unable to move, as if their feet were nailed to the floor. Cheryl's eyes widened and her jaw dropped. A sudden coldness enveloped Marty that made his knees wobble.

The clerk dug his fingers into his temples. He shook his head violently as if it would explode. "I'll kill you all." He flailed his arms, knocking down the cigar display on the counter, smashing the lottery ticket dispenser, and then he grabbed the coffee pot and hurled it at his customers.

It shattered on the floor, spraying Marty and Cheryl with hot coffee, which spurred Marty into action. "Cheryl, get the kids out of here."

She ducked more flying debris and snatched up the children.

The boy clung to his mother's arm. "No. No. Mom...Mom."

His sister, a couple years older, grabbed the boy's wrist. "We have to go. She'll be alright."

Cheryl pulled the kids to the front door and they fled the store.

The husband helped his wife up. She was wobbly on her feet and had a massive welt on her head. Neither noticed the clerk leap over the counter.

"Look out!" Marty yelled.

The clerk flattened the husband with a body-slam. The mother staggered back. Fleeing customers knocked over Marty's shopping cart and a display of potato chips. He jumped into the fray to wrench the psychopath away from the man, but the maniac chomped down on the man's arm and tore out a chunk of meat.

He screamed. "Get him off me!"

"Stop!" Marty kicked the clerk in the head, but he laughed with malevolent glee as blood dripped from his mouth.

"Is that the best you got?" He growled.

"How's this?" Marty kicked him in the ribs.

The clerk howled.

What the hell happened to this guy?

Marty helped the husband get up. "Let's go!"

They ran outside, leaving the clerk to destroy the store, shoving over shelves, spilling inventory, and slamming down aisles with the fury of a wrecking ball.

Cheryl was clutching the kids in the lighted parking lot. They sprinted to their parents. "Mom! Dad!" The mother held her forehead, and the welt looked a little more bruised than before. The father winced, cradled his arm, and squeezed the wound, trying to stop the blood-flow.

The husband turned to Marty and Cheryl. "Thanks for your help in there."

"What could cause someone to get bonkers like that?"

"He seemed fine when we first got in line, then his eye started twitching and he started talking to himself."

"Take care of that arm, and get some ice for your wife's head."

"I'll be fine." His eye twitched. "It's not as bad as it looks, but I can't believe that guy bit me."

Sirens shrieked in the distance. "Someone must've called 911. The cops will be here soon."

The family got into their minivan and tore away.

The convenience store door banged open. The door's bell rang and then clattered on the ground. The maniac clerk lumbered out, scowling and his fists were clenched. Blood burbled from his lips and dribbled from his chin. His wild eyes zeroed in on Marty. "There you are."

Marty shuddered. "Oh, God."

The clerk stomped toward him. "You can't escape me."

Marty grabbed Cheryl. "Come on. We'll get milk and eggs somewhere else."

They fled to the car, got in, and locked the doors. Howls and screams filled the streets. "What the hell is going on around here."

"Just go," Cheryl shouted.

Across the street, a man was running...and two guys were chasing him. Streetlights revealed their bloody faces, and all down the front of their tshirts, more blood...and the three were headed for the convenience store. An SUV careened into the parking lot and slammed into the front wall. Bloody maniacs spilled out, and the small crowd of customers took off running, the maniacs in hot pursuit.

Marty started the car and slammed it into reverse. The maniac clerk leaped onto the hood with the agility of a long jumper and punched a fist into the windshield, spider webbing the glass.

Marty's heart walloped with horror.

"Marty! Get us out of here!"

He gunned the engine. "Hold on." The car whipped a dizzying reverse semicircle, yet the inertia didn't throw the clerk off. He kept smashing his fist into the windshield until his hand broke through, and he started grasping for Marty's face with bloody fingers.

He slammed the shifter into drive and floored the gas. Tires screamed, and he spun the steering wheel to throw the car into a skid. The momentum propelled the attacker over the fender and onto the ground. As the body tumbled and kicked up dust, the hand, severed at the wrist, continued clutching its bloody fingers.

Cheryl screamed.

Marty punched the hand out of the windshield, and as it bounced off the hood, he floored the accelerator, and the car fishtailed onto the road. A glance to the rearview mirror revealed the clerk running after the car as it sped away.

"What the hell was that?" Cheryl cried.

"Your new boyfriend." He leered at her.

"Watch where you're going, smartass."

His heart raced as he accelerated toward their house. He gripped the wheel as he made a sharp turn around a corner. His eyes darted from side to side along the barren streets, searching for any more maniacs. What the hell was happening out there? Before he could think any further, two men rushed out at him from the shadows. They loomed in front of the car, screamed at him, and raised their clenched fists with inexhaustible brutality, trying to block his path. His heart constricted into a frozen fist. Cheryl shrieked in terror. He gunned the gas to the floor and mowed down the maniacs like bowling pins, snapping and crunching bones as the car barreled over them. Howls and groans reverberated from behind as he sped down the street toward home.

There, he skidded the car into their driveway. As soon as he shut off the engine, screams and howls could be heard, coming from somewhere down the block. They jumped out and bolted for the front door. His hands shook as he fumbled with the keys.

"Come on, Marty. Hurry up."

"I'm trying." He dropped the keys.

"Jesus Christ. Can't you do anything right?"

Down on his knees, he groped for the keys. Howls and screams echoed throughout the neighborhood. His heart raced so fast that his chest tightened as if he were on the verge of cardiac arrest, then: "Got 'em."

"It's about time. You're going to get us killed."

"Shut up, Cheryl. You're not helping right now." He unlocked the door, and they scrambled inside. He locked the deadbolt and leaned his back against the door. His breaths came out in spurts. "That was close."

Cheryl turned on the lights in the hallway and the living room, then she ran to Marty and hugged him. Her body was a mass of quivering gelatin. "Marty...what's...happening? I'm scared."

He moved her back a step so he could look at her face-to-face. Her eyes were red and swollen as tears poured down her cheeks. "We'll figure this out."

"I'm sorry about earlier. Sometimes I can be such a bitch."

"I know."

"We could have been killed."

"That's still highly possible. I'm going to turn on the news to see what's going on. In the meantime, close the window blinds and make sure the place is locked up solid."

"I'm on it."

While Cheryl raced through the house, Marty turned the flat screen to CNN. Nothing. Fox. Nothing. He slumped on the couch, leaned forward and wiped sweat from his brow. CBS. *Special Report.* "Here we go."

HEALTH EMERGENCY DECLARATION.

"Cheryl, come sit down."

She sat next to him and squeezed his hand. "Everything's secure."

A woman newscaster wearing a grim face sat at the news desk. "This just in from the New York Center for Disease Control and Prevention. They've declared a public health warning over the outbreak of a novel virus. It affects the central nervous system, turning ordinary citizens into raving mutants. Scientists are calling it the rage virus. There is much we don't know, and as this is a fluid situation, the threat of infection in the greater New York City metropolis is very low, so everyone should remain calm until we get more information. Meanwhile, stay inside after sunset."

Marty felt an icy coldness slide through his bones. He fell back onto the couch and rubbed his temples. "Rage virus? What the hell is this world coming to?"

"What are we going to do?"

"Stay calm."

"Stay calm? You heard them out there. Something's terribly wrong."

He turned off the TV. "How about dinner? I'm starving."

"I don't feel like cooking."

"Can you open a can of spaghetti and meat

balls?"

"Camping food?"

"Why not?"

Cheryl sulked to the kitchen, got out a can of Chef Boyardee then opened up a few drawers. "Where did you put the can opener?"

"Check the utility drawer on the left."

"A hammer, screwdriver...Ah, found it."

She shuddered and dropped the can opener.

Marty gripped her shoulders. "Are you okay?"

She avoided his eyes and wrung her hands. "Do I look okay?" Tears welled in her eyes, and her lips quivered. "We're screwed. This entire world is going to hell, Marty. I'm scared. How are we going to survive?"

He hugged her close. "Calm down."

"What if the mutants find us?"

"I don't know, Cheryl. I have as much information as you."

"We should get out of here. Go to your parents' house in the mountains upstate. Maybe it's safer there."

"We shouldn't go out after sunset. If we run into mutants, they would kill us in a second. We barely escaped the store."

"You're right." She glanced at the floor. "I hope that family made it home alright."

He held her chin up. "Do you know you're beautiful when you're frightened?"

She wiped a tear from her cheek. "Sweet talk isn't going to fix this, Marty."

He kissed her, a quick reassuring kiss on her trembling lips, then to lighten the mood: "Let's eat."

While she heated the spaghetti and meatballs in a pan on the stove, Marty set the table: two bowls, two forks, and two glasses, lit the centerpiece candle, and then added a bottle of scotch he'd saved for a special occasion.

She brought in the steaming pan of camping food and filled the bowls. "I wish we had a time machine that could take us back before all this shit happened."

"This scotch should help us sleep tonight." He held up the bottle. "Look good?"

"What are we celebrating?"

"Our survival."

"In that case, pour the drinks."

They sat, and Marty poured the scotch. He raised the glass to his nose and sniffed. "I'm getting hints of peat, grass, and fruit."

"You're a true connoisseur, Marty."

Someone started pounding on the front door. He damn near dropped his glass. "What the hell?"

A small voice outside shouted, "Let me in. Please, let me in."

Marty's pulse raced. "Sounds like a kid."

Cheryl shot out of her chair and hurried for the door, but Marty intercepted her and grabbed her arm. "What do you think you're doing?"

She struggled to free her arm from his grip. "It's that boy, Marty, from the store. We need to let him in."

"He might be a mutant by now."

The pounding continued. "Hurry. They're coming."

She broke free and rushed to the door. "He needs our help."

Marty followed her. "Oh, for Christ's sake." He ran around her and beat her to the door. "Let me open it."

The bashing against the door became more

frantic.

Marty unlocked the door. "Stay back, Cheryl."

"Just open it."

His heart thwacked against his sternum as he slowly opened the door.

A blonde boy with ruffled hair, ripped clothes, and dirt all over his face stood in the moonlight, panting on the doorstep. His eyes darted about fearfully." Let me in. They're coming."

"Cheryl, you're right. It's the boy from the convenience store. Looks like he's been through hell." He opened the door fully. "Hurry, get in."

The boy bolted inside, and Cheryl took him in her arms. "You're safe now. Where's your sister?"

"I don't know. We split up."

"What about your parents?"

"Dad was driving super fast. Mom was crying her eyes out, sis was screaming. We only got a few blocks from the store when Dad's head started twitching and his eyes got wild. He said he loved us very much, but his voice was all dry and scratchy, then he started laughing like a crazy man. Mom started yelling at him to slow down, but he screamed at her and slapped her in the face."

"Dear Jesus." Cheryl's face was a mask of terror.

The boy's breath came out in hitches. "The car was swerving all over the road. Mom grabbed the wheel. Dad screamed, 'Don't touch me.' His head kept tilting and twisting to the left and the right."

Marty gasped. *Just like the store clerk.*

The boy's eyes were red and tears streamed down his face. "He crashed the car into the garage door, growled like a dog...then he grabbed Mom and bit her neck. Blood sprayed everywhere." The boy buried his face into his hands and sobbed. "The last thing she said was, 'Run, kids, run.'"

Marty's stomach clenched.

Cheryl slapped a hand over her mouth. *No child should witness such horror.*

"We got out and ran."

A knot formed in Marty's stomach. He looked up and down the block. Trees swayed in the cool breeze. Lights were off in his neighbor's houses. No mutants were in sight, but he heard a faint howl in the distance. A thought wormed its way into his brain. The mutant store clerk could be prowling the neighborhood looking for them right now. Marty slammed and locked the door. "You said they're coming. How many are there?"

"Give him a break, Marty." Cheryl led the boy to the dining room table. "Are you hungry? Want some food?"

The boy scowled at the spaghetti and meatballs. "You call that food?"

Cheryl extended her hand to her untouched bowl. "It's either this or Spam." She handed him her fork.

The boy wolfed down the mushy pasta, got sauce smeared on his chin.

She got him a glass of water.

Marty sat next to him and leaned in close. "How did you find us?"

"All the other houses are dark. I knew someone was home here, with all the lights on. Didn't know it was you guys."

Cheryl wiped the boy's saucy face. "Where's the last place you saw your sister?"

"Not far. The mutant's tried to surround us, but we escaped. She ran left past a house with a white fence. I ran right." He bit his lip. "She's out there somewhere."

"There are a lot of white fences in this neighborhood." Cheryl turned to Marty. "We have to go out and find her."

He huffed so hard the centerpiece candle flame flickered. "Are you insane? We won't last a minute—"

"We can't just leave her out there."

"We'll search for her in the morning. At least then we'll have some light. Meanwhile, drink your scotch and heat up the Spam."

"She might not survive until morning."

"We'll have to take that chance." Marty took his own advice and swigged from his glass of scotch.

Cheryl turned to the boy. "Where did you see her last?"

The boy's brow furrowed. "Just a couple blocks...by the white fence, a really tall white fence."

"See, Marty. The Bradberry's place. They painted their stockade fence white. We can get the girl quick and hurry back."

"Absolutely not. We're sure to run into a horde

of them bastards. I don't have a gun or a baseball bat to fight them off. We could end up dead, real easy."

Cheryl stood up and got the hammer from the utility drawer. "What about this?"

"Hand-to-hand combat? Against mutants? Are you kidding me?"

"Fine. I'll find her myself." She headed for the front door, hammer in hand, ready to defeat the enemy to save the girl.

Marty rushed after her and grabbed her arm. "Cheryl, stop. You'll get killed."

She yanked free of his grip. "I can't let a helpless child get slaughtered. Maybe you can." She unlocked the dead bolt.

"Cheryl, wait." He grabbed the hammer from her hand. "At least look out a window to see if it's safe to open the door." He relocked the dead bolt.

Cheryl pulled back the front window curtain. "You're right. There's a group of them milling around in the street."

As Marty reached Cheryl's side, a fist exploded through the window, shattering glass, and a pale hand snatched Cheryl's wrist.

She screamed in terror. An ashen face with black circles around its eyes scowled through the jagged opening. "Gotcha." It was the store clerk.

She fought to free herself from the vise-like grip of a creature so far from human existence it may as well have been an alien from another galaxy. "Marty!"

Before he could pull her away from the window, the mutant bit down hard on Cheryl's arm. Gnarly teeth drew blood.

The horde moved toward the house, suddenly energized and filled with rage. A frosty hand of dread broke into Marty's ribcage and squeezed his pounding heart.

Cheryl howled in agony. "Marty. Help me."

He swung the hammer. Steel met cranium bone with splintering force, but the beast wouldn't release her arm.

Bodies slammed against the front door, busting through the hollow wood, and other mutants smashed through other windows as a cacophony of howls reverberated like hounds from the bowels of Hell. Splinters of wood, shards of glass, and torn draperies were scattered on the living room floor.

Marty delivered another cranial blow to the mutant gnawing on Cheryl's arm. The hammerhead broke through to brain matter but had no effect on the bastard.

A mutant who'd broken in from the back staggered through the dining room and knocked over the table. The centerpiece candle ignited a scrap of drapery on the floor. An inferno was in the making.

Marty turned to the boy. "Kid, get out of here."

The boy dashed up the stairs as flames licked the railing and set the wood and carpet ablaze. Smoke billowed up and fanned out across the ceiling as fire consumed the furniture, curtains, and mutants alike.

Cheryl's attacker looked up at Marty and snapped its teeth together. Marty struck the hammer across its mouth, turning its teeth to Chiclets, but it still wouldn't let go of her bleeding arm. He slammed the hammer into the beast's wrist. Bones cracked. The mutant finally released its grip on Cheryl and fell backwards out the window. She moaned and crumpled to the floor, clutching her wounded and bloody arm and screaming like a banshee.

Pale arms and grasping hands reached in through the broken window, and Marty got busy with the hammer, attacking each mutant that attempted to enter the house. The mutants screamed and howled, not in pain, but in a rage, a bloodlust that defied all reasoning, as if their victims' deaths were the only thing in the world that mattered.

Then there was an amplification of sounds that shook Marty's soul. Pounding on the walls and doors merged with Cheryl's screams, the howling of beasts, the crackling of flames, all reverberating and increasing until the entire house was thrashing, hammering, banging and screeching. The heat was intense.

Marty felt sheer terror seize him, heat and fear, a toxic brew that threatened to bowl him over, but they had to escape. Running outside was out of the question. Fleeing upstairs seemed futile, too, as heat and fire and smoke would rise to eventually kill them, however, it might buy him a little time to figure out his next move.

He grabbed Cheryl's good arm. "Come on. We have to go."

She wrenched away from his grip with surprising strength. Her head wobbled from side to side, and her body shook in a paroxysm of demented fury. "I'm not going anywhere with you, you liar. I saw the way you looked at pink-tights." She glowered at him with the same ghastly pallor and darkened circles around the eyes as the other mutants.

The flesh on the nape of Marty's neck crawled and his hand tightened on the hammer, but he couldn't bring himself to bash in her brains. "Oh no. Not you, Cheryl."

"You're next, cheater." She snickered with a gleeful grin.

Mutants broke through the wall of fire and poured in through the broken door and windows. The store clerk suddenly loomed next to Cheryl, her blood still dripping from his broken-toothed maw. She was one of them now, and he had taken claim to her. No hammer, no bullet, no weapon could ever undo that damage.

Marty turned and bolted up the smoke-filled

staircase, shoes catching fire and his heart pounding as the mutants raced up after him. At the top of the stairs, the smoke was thick in his throat as he dashed down the hallway and burst into the master bedroom. He locked the door behind him and kicked fire from his feet. The stink of his singed hair sickened his stomach.

The horde banged against the door. It shook and bowed under the tremendous pressure.

On the other side of the room, the boy strained at the window, trying to slide up the lower pane. He turned to Marty; his eyes were big as silver dollars. "Help me, mister. Hurry."

Marty bounded past the bed and dresser. "I'm coming, kid." He reached the window.

"It's stuck."

"Let me try."

Behind him, the mutants busted down the door and scrambled toward Marty and the boy, screaming and yelling with their fists pumping air.

"Don't let them escape," Cheryl shouted. "Rip them to shreds."

Marty freed the stuck window and shoved it

upwards then pushed the kid out onto a narrow ledge. "Run, boy, and good luck." Then he closed the window.

"What are you doing?"

Marty whirled with the hammer raised at the throng of mutants. Before he could get in a single swing, they overwhelmed and battered him until death took him to a better place.

Chapter Two

Fire consumed the house, and black smoke spiraled into the moonlit night sky. The boy hung off the ledge and dropped to the ground. He bolted into the darkness as the screams and howls of marauding mutants echoed throughout Montrose.

Cheryl's voice rose above the mayhem. "We'll find you, little boy, and your sister too."

The eye-burning stench of burned wood shot up his nostrils as he backed away from the burning house. Amid the snapping wood of collapsing walls, the mutants' howls and cackles reverberated from the inferno. Several mutants, their clothes ablaze and skin as blackened as charred meat, staggered from the raging inferno and fell to the ground where they shriveled and died. One of them noticed him, glowered and stabbed a burning finger at him before it collapsed.

Cheryl appeared, unscathed, and roared, "There he is."

Other mutants howled and snarled then raced after him like a pack of wolves, their teeth snapping.

Oh no. A lump formed in his throat. Fear locked his knees, even as he ordered his feet to flee. He had to find his sister. They had to survive. *Go. Before it's too late.*

He raced away, arms pumping, legs churning, but the horde of mutants cut the distance in half as they chased him down the street. He passed several houses, trying to remember which way his sister went.

She ran left by the white fence.

He careened left, tripped on a skateboard, hopped over a rail fence, and ducked down a back alley. A tall white fence came out of the gloom. *Yes, this looks familiar. Sis went this way.*

In the distance, sirens wailed.

He climbed a six-foot stockade fence and dropped into someone's back yard.

Seconds later, the horde of mutants busted through the rail fence and poured into the alley.

Ducking down in the bushes, he shifted his eyes back and forth, looking for a place to hide. A lone tree towered over the yard, and dim moonlight illuminated a tree house high up in its branches. *They'll never find me up there.*

He bolted to a rope ladder and started climbing up. It wasn't as easy as it looked, but he made it to a small platform then pulled up the ladder. Only now could he catch his breath, leaned against the tree house wall, and scanned the alley. From here he could see the mutants rage past the stockade fence. Staying low, he scooted to the doorway and crawled inside.

"Don't hurt me," a girl's voice cried out from the darkness.

His heart flailed in the cold grip of terror, then recognition. "Sis?"

"Billy?"

"Thank God I found you."

"You're alive."

They groped in the darkness and finally embraced each other.

Chapter Three

1n Crotonville, Kevin Tippler slumped on his couch in his townhouse in Mystic Estates, a gated community on the banks of the Hudson River. It boasted heated pools, tennis courts, a clubhouse, and jitney service to the train station. He'd earned this luxury lifestyle, working for Vericom Wireless Communications, well, more like slaving for his boss, Frank Cicero. However, tonight, Frank was the least of his problems. On the television, CNN, ABC, NBC...they all droned on about an outbreak, some kind of rage virus, in Montrose, five miles to the north, up the Hudson.

Kevin switched to News 12 Westchester. At the bottom of the screen, a scrolling banner read: *Video shows violent fight at Montrose convenience store.* A blonde news anchor said, "Police have released a new video of a wild and vicious fight inside a Save More Store. Investigators are searching for the clerk who brutally attacked his customers. Police need your help to find the perpetrator." The video switched to a bearded face. "Here's a picture of the missing clerk. If you see this man, call 911 immediately. Do not engage."

Kevin's throat tightened. He flipped channels to ABC News where they broadcasted a video of a house on fire. In the studio, "This is David Gibson with Breaking News from Montrose, a sleepy hamlet in Westchester County, which is the scene of a horrific, brutal attack on a single-family home. Witnesses claim men and women with ashen faces and dark circles around their eyes attacked this residence, killing the homeowner before the horde ran into the darkness. Some claimed they were chasing a young boy who'd fled the scene. Westchester County Police engaged a mob running from an alley. Shots were fired. Casualties are unknown at this time, but several fugitives are still at large."

The camera zoomed out to reveal a man with white hair and wearing a pinstriped suit and red tie, sitting next to Gibson. "This is infectious disease expert Doctor James Salkland."

He nodded to the camera.

"Doctor, what can you tell us about these attacks? Are they related to the rage virus we've heard about?"

The doctor steepled his fingers. "There's speculation about a virus in the air or water, but we're unsure about the extent or what is causing everyday citizens to go berserk. The outbreaks are rare and isolated, so the threat to New York City is relatively low. Go Yankees."

Fighting panic, Kevin turned off the TV. He had plans to take his son, Ethan, to the game tomorrow night. Corin might be freaked out about all this nonsense and not let him go. He picked up his cell phone and called his wife.

"What do you want, Kevin?"

"We're still on for the Yankees game tomorrow night, right? Me and Ethan?"

"No chance in hell you're taking our son anywhere at night."

"Why not?"

"Haven't you been watching the news, or don't they care about the Rage virus at Rory Dolan's Pub?"

"Ha ha, very funny. You should have been a comedian. The CDC doesn't know squat. Punk kids are just pranking a neighborhood in Montrose. It's all a bunch of hype for the ratings war. There's nothing to worry about."

"I'm worried that you'll get drunk, as usual, and I don't want Ethan to be around you."

"I won't drink at the game."

"Yeah, right, Kevin. You're full of shit. You can't help yourself with all those beer vendors circling you like buzzards looking for dead meat. And that's what you are to me, Kevin, dead meat. You'll be wasted by the third inning. By the fifth inning, you won't even know your son is there, and if you make it to the ninth inning, you'll get arrested for drunken disorderly."

Kevin ran his hands through his hair. "Jesus, Corin, take it easy. What crawled up your ass? Ethan is my son. I have rights too, ya know."

"You lost your rights when you chose the bottle over your family."

Kevin's stomach churned with anguish. "I've stopped drinking, alright? Give me another chance."

"I don't trust you with our only child."

Kevin's hopes sank. "I've been a good father."

"When you're drinking, not so much. I'm sorry, but it's the truth."

Kevin heard Ethan in the background.

"Mom, is that Dad?"

"It's your father. He's not good enough to be a dad."

Ow. That hurt. "Corin, let me speak to him, please."

"Make it quick."

Kevin's hopes rose.

"Hey. Whatcha doing, Dad?"

He swallowed hard. *I want to give you the biggest hug.* "I miss you, buddy."

"I miss you too. Mom says I can't go to the game—"

"Forget about that. I got two tickets with our names on them."

"Then I'm going with you?"

"Does a bear got teeth?"

"Yeah. It's gonna be awesome. The Judge is the man. Can't wait to see him blast one out of the park. I love you so much. Hey, Mom, Dad's taking me to the Yankees game tomorrow."

"Gimme that phone." She got on the line. "What did I say?"

"You can't say no. Do you hear how happy he is?"

"Kevin, You're an alcoholic, a bad example for your son, and besides, it's too dangerous to go out at night."

"Do you really want to break the boy's heart?"

"Sure, if it saves him from you and that doomsday virus out there. He's safer with me."

"Doomsday. Do you hear yourself? I promise he'll be alright."

"Promise? Did you join AA like you promised? No. You didn't."

"I will soon. I promise."

"Your promises don't mean shit, Kevin. I've heard it before. And you can't promise a dangerous virus isn't going to get him killed."

"Relax. It'll be safe enough. I'll bring masks, just in case. The first sign of trouble, we're out of there."

"No way. I can't let you endanger our son in a stadium full of fans with that virus going around."

"Mom," Ethan shouted in the background. "If Dad says it's okay. It's okay. Why do you have to be so mean?"

"See what you've done?" Kevin could hear the spit in her voice. "You've turned him against me."

"Easy fix, Corin. Just let him go to the game."

"Are you going to dump all the liquor in the house and attend AA meetings?"

"I'll do it...anything you say."

"Don't let us down again, Kevin, or so help me..."

"Then it's a yes?"

"It's a yes, but don't make me regret it."

He heard Ethan cheering in the background. "Bring my mitt, Dad."

"He wants his mitt."

"I heard. Tell him I'm on it."

"My money is on you forgetting his mitt."

"What happened to you, Corin? What happened to the woman I fell in love with?"

"I'm still here, but the man I loved changed."

"I'll change back. I promise."

"Don't make promises. Make changes."

"I will. See you tomorrow after work...when I

pick up Ethan."

"No stopping off at Rory Dolan's, ya hear."

"Got it."

The call ended.

Excited enough to have a stiff drink in celebration, Kevin rushed upstairs to Ethan's room to get his baseball glove. There sat his Indy 500 racecar bed with a stuffed hippopotamus resting on the pillow. Lego pieces, puzzles, Dr. Seuss books lay about, and Yankees baseball posters of the Judge and Superman filled the walls, painted blue, back during the time Corin was pregnant. All he had now were these memories.

Where is that glove?

He searched high and low until he found it buried under Ethan's pillow. The soft leather smelled of infield clay and outfield grass. He slipped his left hand into the glove and popped his right fist into the leather pocket while memories of Ethan in the Crotonville Little League filled his mind.

Tears welled and his heart plunged. *I hope we can play baseball again, buddy.*

He plodded across the hall to his bedroom and

flumped on the bed. The room seemed so much smaller and the bed seemed so much bigger without Corin.

He could still smell her floral and vanilla perfume on her pillow and remembered how they had rolled around under the sheets. The memory of her lips felt so real yet so far away, and now so cold. Whisky heaven had created this hellish life he was forced to live. He had to win back Corin's better graces.

I must make better choices or lose my family forever, but a drink will make me feel better. Corin will never know.

He clomped down the stairs to the kitchen, opened up the cabinet, and from the top shelf, he took down a bottle of Jim Beam and a rock glass then set it on the kitchen island. His hand shook as he poured the dark booze into the glass. Toasted oak with hints of caramel, cinnamon, and candied apple scents wafted to his nose. "Heaven awaits." He gulped down the bourbon and felt the warm promise of relief slide down his throat. His eyes watered. He shivered and smacked his lips. "That's some good shit."

Shit, what am I doing? I've been clean and sober for almost a month, and I'm pissing it all away. He shrugged. *I'll start a new sobriety streak, and this time go longer without a drink. Tomorrow. I'll start tomorrow.*

He poured another drink, but before he could toss it back, a knock rattled the patio door. *Who could that be? Oh God, it's the mutants.* He hustled to the patio door, heart pounding, and peeked through a chink in the vertical blinds.

There stood his next-door neighbor, Marge Thompson, holding a bottle of Smirnoff Blue vodka and two glasses.

He pressed his lips together. *Shit, what is she doing here? I could let her in, but what would Corin say if she saw me with this vixen? She would kill me. I'll pretend not to be home.*

Marge spotted him behind the blinds and smiled.

Damn, there goes that plan.

He parted the blinds and slid open the patio door.

"Evening, neighbor." The curls at the ends of her auburn locks bounced when she nodded her head. She wore a pink blouse, the buttons straining to contain her round breasts. Her tight jeans seemed painted on her round buttocks and slender legs. The black boots added to her *bad-girl* persona.

Kevin forced his eyes to focus on her face. "What do you think you're doing?"

"Don't be so happy to see me."

"I doubt you're here to borrow a cup of sugar."

Marge peered inside. Her eyebrows rose. "I noticed your wife and son haven't been around lately...figured you'd like some company."

"Corin is at her parents with Ethan."

"Are you just going to just stand there or invite a lady in?"

"It's late and I have to work tomorrow morning."

"This is just a friendly visit."

A little too friendly. Kevin stepped aside. "All right. Just for a minute."

Marge grinned, exposing her perfect white teeth. She strode into the house, her head turning left and right, curls jiggling, then spotted the bottle of Beam. "Hey, what's this? You started the party without me."

"It's just a nightcap before bed."

Marge crossed the kitchen and set the bottle of vodka and glasses next to the Beam. She handed him his glass of bourbon. "Don't let me stop you. Get your drink on."

Kevin took the glass of booze and took a swig.

"That's the spirit."

"It really is getting late, Marge."

Her soft hands caressed his cheek. "I'm just getting started."

Kevin's heart raced at her touch. He pushed her hand away though a part of him didn't want to.

Marge meandered into Kevin's living room. "I like what you've done with the place except..." Then she frowned. "Look how sterile this room looks. Wilted plants. Lights as dim as a prison cell." She wiped her finger along an end table. "Tsk, tsk tsk. Look at all this dust. You need some help." She returned to the kitchen and poured herself a drink.

Kevin's mouth watered as he watched the liquid sunshine gurgle from the bottle and splash into the glass.

She strode up to him. "You could use a lady's touch around here."

"It's not as bad as it looks."

"You're kidding yourself if you think your wife will magically reappear. You need to move on with your life." Marge grinned. "That's where I come in."

Kevin wondered if Corin would ever forgive him for being a drunk and come back home with Ethan. His heart flailed somewhere between hope and fear.

"You must be lonely." She raised her glass in salute.

"I keep busy with work." He acknowledged her toast and slammed back his glass of whiskey.

She followed suit, downed her vodka then licked her red-glossed lips. "You know what they say about all work and no play." She winked. "You wanna play with any of this?"

You're killing me, Marge.

He thought her blouse buttons would pop and let loose her silicone implants. "I have to work in the morning, and I'm taking my son to his first

Yankees game tomorrow night."

"Busy day. No time to play." She poured herself another drink. "Aren't you worried about the outbreak?"

"The news has everyone in a tizzy. Life goes on."

"I hope so." She moved into the living room and settled onto the couch as if she owned the place. "Pour yourself a vodka and come sit with me."

"I got my own, thanks." He elected not to drink any more. Even sober he'd play hell resisting her.

She crossed her legs and patted the sofa. "Let's celebrate Ethan's first baseball game."

Kevin shook his head. "I can't be hung over at work in the morning. My boss is a prick."

"Come on. Stop sulking and join the party. The end of the world is coming." She raised her glass, sloshing out vodka on her hand. "We might as well make the best of it."

Kevin leaned on the kitchen doorway and folded his arms. "You don't give up, do ya?"

"It's one of my best qualities. Persistence.

When I see something I want, I go after it."

Kevin felt his groin tighten. His cheeks flushed. Even from here he could savor the fruity fragrance of her perfume. He imagined he was on an island resort with her, the clear waters of Cancun washing up on the shore as they strolled barefoot in the warm surf, hand-in-hand. He shivered in the ecstasy of his imagination, what a fling he could have with her, but as his thoughts flashed to Corin, he fought to overcome his mounting desire for this temptress. If there were any chance of him getting his family back, Marge was not the right course to follow. "I'm sorry, Marge. It's time to call it a night."

She whimpered. "Are you sure? I'll stay. You won't regret it."

"How about a rain check...maybe during the next apocalypse."

After downing the vodka, she rose from the couch, kind of like the Phoenix rising in all her glory. "Party pooper." She slinked toward him like a feral feline. "You're missing out on a good thing."

"I'm sure you're right." He led her to the patio

door.

"Corin is lucky to have a loyal man like you." Marge gathered up her bottle and glasses.

"Put in a good word for me, will ya?"

"Why did she leave?"

"I'm an alcoholic."

"Could have fooled me. If you change your mind, my door is always open."

"Good night, Marge."

She blew him a kiss, stepped outside, and quickly melded into the darkness.

He closed the door, the blinds, then stepped up to Jim Beam and poured himself another round. Drinking alone was a whole lot less complicated. Tomorrow he'd quit again.

Chapter Four

The Next morning, Kevin found himself fighting rush hour traffic and a hangover that would kill a horse. It was always the same routine. One drink led to two drinks led to three drinks, the next thing he knew, he was shitfaced, lying on his back and watching the room spin. He'd sworn each shot of booze was an antidote for his loneliness, or a jab at Corin for taking Ethan away, or medication to erase the vision of Marge from his brain, when in truth, he drank for the hell of it. And hell is what he got.

He slammed his hand on the steering wheel as the gridlocked traffic on the Saw Mill River Parkway crawled ahead. His boss, the prick that he was, would give him hell if he came in late.

Goddamn. He felt helplessly trapped in traffic. Horns honked. Tempers flared. Commuters shouted. Cars blocked every corner. How many people lived in this area? How many people lived on the earth? Billions. It seemed that everyone was driving to work at the same time as him. He gripped the steering wheel tighter.

Maybe the rage virus wasn't such a bad thing after all. Perhaps it was time to cull the human herd. Get rid of the weak, the ones taking up space, sucking up resources, and not giving anything in return, and especially the ones blocking his way to work. Let natural selection do its job and clean house, but not him, of course. He was an essential worker, providing crucial telecommunications to the masses.

Get out of my way, by God, and let me do my job.

He tried to get off on a side street, a longer way, he knew, but possibly faster, but a pickup truck blocked the exit. "Hey, buddy, get out of the way."

"Screw you, Mac." The muscle-head flipped him the finger. "Wait in line like everyone else."

Kevin edged around the truck, got onto a secondary road, where he stopped at a red light, a million cars back. All he could do was grin and bear it and wish for another drink.

Finally, he skidded into the parking lot of Vericom, a thirty-thousand square foot building nestled in the back of Executive Promenade in Yonkers. At the exact moment he turned off the ignition, it was 9:01am. His heart pounded with dread. *Strike one. I'm late.*

From where he parked, he could see Frank Cicero standing at the front door with his hairy arms folded and foot tapping, a bespectacled man who towered over most men. He wore his salt and pepper hair in a military cut like a drill sergeant in the army. A smoldering cigar dangled from his mouth, and he masticated it back and forth like a praying mantis chewing the head off its mate. His eyes scanned the parking lot as a general would survey a battlefield.

Now Kevin was two minutes late.

Another minute passed before Frank knocked the ash off his cigar on the heel of his boot and stuffed it in his top pocket.

Good. He's going inside. Kevin wouldn't have to face him, just yet.

Frank put on a white mask.

Kevin slapped a hand over his mouth. He'd

gotten a text memo that morning. The company, as a precaution, ordered all employees to wear masks. *Shit. I forgot. Strike two.* Sweat broke out on his forehead. He'd have to face the music. He got out of the car and trudged toward the front door with his head lowered.

Fat lot a good that did.

"Hold it right there, Tippler." Cicero looked at his watch. "You're late."

Kevin stopped and looked up. "Sorry, boss. Traffic was a bear. Big accident at the Saw Mill. Nothing I could do."

"Do you think I care to hear some bullshit story about why you're late? I don't pay you to be late."

"The company pays me, Frank, and not near enough to put up with the likes of you."

"Where's your mask?"

Kevin rubbed his neck. "Sorry, forgot to get one."

"The company pays you to wear a mask."

"They pay me to do my job, besides, there are no alerts for this area. All the trouble's up north."

Frank stuck his nose in Kevin's face, so close he

could smell cigar-breath. "Wrong answer. I don't want my employees to get the virus. Get out of here and don't come back without a mask."

"There's no way I'm fighting that traffic again."

"If you want to get paid, you better get a mask."

"Give me a break, Frank. Security will have extra masks. I'll bring my own next time." He stepped around him to head for the door.

Frank blocked him. "You're a screw-up, Kevin. Not sure why Vericom hired you in the first place. You're a cockroach that slipped through the cracks. HR dropped the ball."

Kevin stood tall. "I've been here twenty years. Do you know how many problems I've solved for this company? I lost count. How many outages that I've helped fix?"

"But you can't show up for work on time."

"This company needs me, so don't bust my balls over a couple of minutes."

Two younger employees rushed by them, sipping their coffee as they entered the building without masks.

Kevin pointed at them. "Hey, what about those guys? Why aren't you busting their balls?"

"They're not losers like you."

Blood boiled in Kevin's veins. "I'm going to call my union rep and report you for harassment. File a grievance against you. I'm sure your boss will be happy about that."

Cicero put his hands up. "Hold on, chief. Don't threaten me. Save your energy for your job." He pulled out a mask from his pocket and shoved it at him. "Wear this, you sorry excuse for an employee."

"Gee thanks, Frank. You're a good human being, after all."

"Don't take my charity for weakness. Be late again and I'll have your ass, and you can cry to the union all you want." He moved aside and scowled. "Now get to work."

Kevin gritted his teeth, slapped on the mask, and stormed inside. He hustled through Vericom's lobby, a veritable fortress of marble, glass, and steel, the vast expanse filled with soft lighting and echoes. The building housed powerful servers, switches, and microprocessors that routed millions of cell phone calls faster than the blink of an eye. His ID badge gave him access to the control room.

During the week, hundreds of technicians and engineers, invisible to the public, operated the consoles, computer terminals, and routers that made expeditious telecommunications attainable. Twenty-five flat-screen LED monitors lined the walls, portraying graphs of traffic flow in various frequencies and regions. One screen displayed the entire fiber optic highway that streamed calls at the speed of light. Engineers could interpret raw data glitches and manipulate or restore the flow as needed.

He was one of those engineers, the only tech on duty this Saturday while the others worked remotely or had the weekend off. Sitting at his terminal, he grumbled then keyed in his code to gain access to Vericom's servers.

"Good morning, Kevin."

The calendar came up on-screen. *"Yankees Game - 7pm."*

He smiled. Tonight he was taking Ethan to his first Yankees game. His son was stoked. His mom, not so much. Their separation sucked, but he hoped someday they'd get back together.

He took out the Yankees tickets from his suit coat pocket and admired them like precious jewels. *Left field seats. Right to the spot where The Judge could blast out a home run.*

He set the tickets next to his keyboard, clicked off the calendar, and loaded his switch assignments. A list of router upgrades and pending maintenance scrolled down the screen. He'd be lucky to get out there by 4pm.

The control room door opened, and in walked Frank.

"Now what?" Kevin muttered.

Frank clapped his hands, and sure enough, he strode to Kevin's terminal and peered over his shoulder. "Looks like you've got a lot of work to do. Don't bother taking any coffee breaks."

Kevin adjusted his mask. "You don't have to stand over my shoulder. I know what I'm doing."

"You're the best we've got, Kevin. That's why you're going to work during the big Yankees game tonight."

"What?"

"You have to make sure the network is performing at its optimum level, especially against the dreaded Red Sox."

"I'm not working tonight."

"You are if I say you are. We don't want any customer complaints now, do we?"

Kevin's bloodstream took a shot of hot adrenaline. He spun his swivel chair around and pulled down his mask. "We have on-call people for that. My shift ends at four."

"Not today, it doesn't." Frank folded his arms. "You were late. You owe me, mister."

Heat burned up the back of Kevin's neck. "It's my son's first Yankees game. I'm not going to disappoint him."

"Tell him his daddy forgot his mask and shouldn't have been late for work. Your boss grounded you."

"There's no way I'm missing that game."

"Listen, old man. I've been hearing rumors about the company laying people off, some with a buyout package. You should take it. Enjoy your golden years."

"I should, but you're not getting rid of me that

easily. I still got plenty of fuel in the tank and plan on working for a long time."

Frank chuckled as if Fuck-with-Kevin was his favorite game. "Either quit or get fired."

"No way. You're not pushing me out so you can put in some younger guy who'll work for less money."

"You know that's not legal, Kevin. Age discrimination can rack up a huge Federal fine. Either way, you'll have a hard time proving you were forced out." Frank laughed. "Hell of a choice you've got to make. Your job or baseball." His eyes locked on the tickets, and he snatched them up. "Hey, not bad. Good seats."

"Put them down, Frank."

He stuffed the tickets in his top pocket, right next to his stinking cigar. "You won't be needing these."

Kevin shot up out of the chair. "Hey, you can't do that. Give 'em back, or..."

"Or you'll do what? Quit?"

"Every dog gets his day, Frank, and I hope to be there when you get yours."

"Tough talk for an old man."

Jim Keane

"I'm not old."

"I'll make you a deal. You take care of all these upgrades and the maintenance chores..." He pointed to the data scrolling down the screen, "and maybe I'll let you get out of here on time."

"This isn't Let's Make a Deal. I want those tickets back."

"Just do your job—"

"You're a prick, Frank. You know that? If I checked, I bet I wouldn't find a heart beating in your chest."

"Four o'clock...job done, or no tickets. Deal?"

"Fine." Kevin slumped back into his chair and lowered his head. No wonder this job drove him to drink and screwed up his marriage.

Frank gloated over him for a few minutes then left, laughing behind his mask.

Kevin tore off his mask and tossed it on the counter. "Prick."

Chapter Five

Frank Cicero tromped into his large office and slammed the door behind him. On his massive desk, he'd situated two phones and four flat-screen monitors so he could constantly oversee the network remotely. A wooden conference table with ten chairs were set up across the room, and a blue yoga mat lay on the floor. He flumped into his chair and took off his mask, still fuming over that arrogant ass, Kevin the Screwup. If a shrink were to diagnose this anger, he'd say Frank's emotions were misplaced. He was actually angry at the world and at God over the loss of his wife, Elizabeth.

With auburn hair and blue eyes, she'd stunned him the first time they'd met. They'd dated, fell in love, got married: she'd changed his life, but now she was gone forever. He remembered Our Lady of Mercy hospital where he'd gripped Elizabeth's hand in an ICU ward decorated with love: big balloons tethered to her bed swayed and read: GET WELL SOON and WE LOVE YOU. A glass vase of yellow roses sat on her bedside table, but the damned bitter antiseptic odors of soaps and cleaners overpowered the fragrance of the flowers. Harsh fluorescent lighting lit the room. Nurses hurried through the hallways. In this world of medicine and miracles, the call of the grim reaper was omnipresent for his Elizabeth.

A clear plastic tube trickling a solution from an I-V bag was attached to a needle in her arm. Wires to a heart monitor snaked from her frail chest. Slow beeps from the machine plodded along, echoing in the room.

The patter of rain drummed outside.

Elizabeth curled up in her bed, unmoving. A sticky film covered her half-closed eyes. Her once shiny head of auburn hair was now bald, and her body was gaunt. She breathed with a harsh, rattling sound. Her face was grey.

Frank squeezed her cold and clammy hand. "Hang in there, baby."

Elizabeth licked her chapped lips. "So...tired. I...must...look...terrible."

Frank frowned and his lip trembled. "I only see the woman I married. Nothing else. You're still perfect." He gave her a sip of water. She gagged on it. Something as simple as swallowing was nearly impossible. "You should try to eat something."

Elizabeth crinkled her nose. "Everything tastes so bitter."

"You have to keep up your stamina."

"I'm dying, Frank. Why bother?"

His heart fluttered at the thought. "Don't say that."

"You know it's true."

"You can't think like that. You'll be alright."

"Use your eyes. Do I look alright?"

"You can't give up."

"That's easy for you to say."

"What do you want me to say?"

"I'm sorry, Frank. I don't know what I want."

"It's okay. I know you don't want to die."

Elizabeth grimaced, her face a mask of agony. Sweat glistened on her pale forehead. She squeezed her eyes shut.

Frank's heart rate surged. "Let me get the

nurse to give you more pain killers." He hurried to the hallway, darting his eyes until he found a nurse and grabbed her by the arm. "My...wife. You got to help her."

The nurse's eyebrows shot up. "What's wrong?"

"She's in a lot of pain."

"I'll be right in."

"Hurry."

The nurse administered more morphine into Elizabeth's IV drip.

After a while, the lines of anguish etched into Elizabeth's forehead dissipated.

"Call me if you need anything else."

"Thanks so much."

The nurse left.

Frank squeezed Elizabeth's hand. "How do you feel?"

"Sleepy."

Frank put his hand on her forehead. "Now, just rest."

"What are you going...to do without me?"

"Don't say such things. You're going to beat this cancer. You're a fighter. So fight."

"But what if I don't?"

Frank blinked back tears. "You will, dammit. You have to."

Elizabeth's eyelids fluttered like the wings of a bird soaring skyward. "I love you, Frank..."

"I love you too, sweetheart."

"Frank, where are you?"

He leaned forward and gripped her hand tighter. "I'm right here, Elizabeth."

The heart monitor flat-lined.

No, no, no. Frank's heart thumped with dread. He couldn't catch a breath and struggled to speak. "Nurse. Nurse, come quickly."

The nurses rushed into the room. There was nothing they could do.

He felt as though his heart had been ripped from his chest.

***

Now, in his imagination, Frank heard his wife say: *"Why do you have to be such a prick, Frank?"*

"Because you're not here. I need you."

"You need to move on. Find someone to love. Torturing your employee isn't going to help."

"But it helps keep my mind off of losing you.

Work is all I have now." He shook his head as tears welled. "It's not fair."

"I know. Who said life was fair, anyway?"

"If I can't be happy, nobody else can." Frank squeezed Kevin's Yankees tickets, wanting to tear them to shreds, to deny Kevin the happiness they'd bring him and his son.

"Don't do it, Frank."

Breathe, he told himself and closed his eyes. His heart rolled in an ocean of despair.

He placed his palms together and put them close to his chest. *Namaste. You must breathe. Remember your yoga practice.*

I don't want to breathe. Yoga doesn't matter to me. I want to fire Kevin, make him miserable, make him want to die.

When Frank entirely gave in to his yoga routine and freed his mind from Elizabeth, he could feel his heartbeat and breathing slow down. However, getting to that Zen point proved cumbersome and nearly impossible.

Breathe dammit.

He felt his face get hot. His anxiety level was about to go nuclear. He had to calm down, find peace and tranquility, and for that, he kept the yoga mat nearby.

He changed into sweat pants and a sweatshirt, and then in his stocking-clad feet, he stepped onto the mat and started with the mountain pose to calm his breathing and attain balance. Then the downward-facing dog, he held that for a few minutes, then he assumed the warrior pose, arms up, right foot front, then left foot front, arms out, right knee bend, left knee bend. Repeat.

After ten minutes, he broke a sweat. With every pose and every stretch, he became more limber and calmer. His mind went to mountain streams and the smell of high pines and rich earth. He pushed himself harder and exerted his body to the breaking point. The half-moon pose did him in, his coupe de grace. He winced as he felt a dull pain in his back. It turned to a throb then an ache, and his throat tightened as he attempted to straighten and stand upright. His left thigh cramped and he toppled to the mat. That damned Kevin Tippler. Frank blamed this painful muscle pull on that slacker, as well, a transgression that wouldn't go unpunished.

Chapter Six

At 3:59 p.m., Kevin performed an admin save on a Nokia router, which finished the configuration changes that would handle the expected extra bandwidth needed during the game tonight. Frank wouldn't have a damn thing to bitch about.

Now he could think about Ethan's bright eyes and wide smile as they headed for the game.

I can't wait to see you, buddy.

He closed out his terminal, donned the mask, and raced for the door. Maybe he could dodge Frank and make it out the front exit unimpeded. He peeked out of the control room door. The hallway was clear all the way to the lobby, but a sudden realization hit him. The tickets.

I can't leave without the tickets.

Panic kicked his heart rate into high gear. He rushed back to his terminal and picked up the phone to call Frank.

Just then, the door opened and Frank barged in. "Going somewhere, Tippler?" His stern voice was muffled behind his mask, but that didn't make it any less irritating. He looked at his watch and shook his head. "It's amazing how punctual you are when you want to leave, but to come to work on time? Not so much."

"Gimme a break, Frank. Everything is done. The cell sites handling Yankee Stadium are performing as cleanly as a well-oiled engine." Kevin held out his hand. "Now, give me my tickets."

Frank canted his eyebrows. "Tickets? What tickets?"

"Don't play dumb with me. I spent a lot of money on those seats."

Frank smirked. "Oh, those tickets."

"Yeah. You stole them from me this morning, or did you conveniently forget?"

"No, my memory is very clear. You were late for work."

Kevin's face heated. "Just give me the tickets."

"How do I know you did your job correctly?"

"Twenty years, Frank. Quit busting my balls."

"Let me see. Run a spreadsheet on the upgrades."

"I gotta get out of here. We'll be late for the first pitch."

"Do it anyway."

Chapter Seven

1t was 5 p.m. when Kevin stormed out of the Vericom building, shaking his head and gripping the Yankees tickets. First one spreadsheet, then two, then Frank made him run systems checks on everything he had done. Anything to burn daylight and get his goat. He felt like a bullied schoolboy cowering under Frank's admonitions as he did what he was told so he could get out of there.

I'm not going to let Frank get the best of me. No way. He'll see. I'll make sure of it.

In the car, he tore off his mask and threw it on the passenger seat. Any other night, after a day like today, he'd buzz on over to Rory Dolan's Pub and sink a few pints, the very thing that got him into trouble with Corin and wrecked his marriage of ten years. But not tonight.

As Kevin sped home, he rode the accelerator with a heavy foot, switching lanes, and he blew through a yellow light to beat the red. He was entering an intersection when some guy in a Chevy Tahoe with gigantic tires shot out in front of him and cut him off. Riding shotgun, a punk with backwoodsman sideburns and a green Mack Truck baseball hat, showed him his middle finger and shouted. "Asshole."

Kevin laid on the horn, and the driver flipped him the middle finger, as well.

"What the hell's wrong with those guys?" He noticed the Tahoe had out-of-state plates and an NRA bumper sticker in the back window. *Damn rednecks.* Still, all of these irritants, along with his ire and contempt at Frank Cicero, couldn't put a dent in his good mood. He was going to the Yankees game with his son.

I'm late getting home. It's all Frank's fault, but life is good.

The driver in the Chevy Tahoe pulled away, and Kevin followed it, weaving through traffic as the lug-heads inside harassed drivers who got in their way. Gotta love New York.

Suddenly, the Tahoe's brake lights lit and the tires blew smoke.

Kevin slammed on the brakes just in time.

The Tahoe lunged forward, and the brake lights came on again.

Kevin had to hit the brakes again. Why the hell were they brake-checking him? He blew the horn at the rednecks, more in frustration than with any belief the gesture would change their behavior. "Learn how to drive, you piece of garbage."

As it turned out, the driver didn't take kindly to being honked at, and when the traffic stopped at a red light, the driver's door flew open, he got out and stormed toward Kevin. At six-foot-five and well over two hundred pounds, the redneck's chest was bigger than most NFL linemen. Worse, there was something wrong with him. Black skin encircled his eyes, and instead of being red with rage, his face was bleached white.

Kevin's stomach knotted.

Now, you did it, you idiot.

He cranked the steering wheel hard-right, accelerated around the Tahoe, and blasted down the shoulder, breaking more traffic laws than he cared to count.

Chapter Eight

A half-hour later, Kevin sped through Mystic Estates' front gate and drove directly to Corin's parents' place, two cul-de-sacs down from their once happy home. He was going to be late for the Yankees game and Ethan would be disappointed.

He parked in front of the duplex, got out, and rushed to the door. Corin was already there, waiting to jump down his throat. The door flew open, and her hooded blue eyes glared at him with the usual disdain. "You're late, Kevin."

"I got tied up in traffic."

"Were you drinking?"

"Some jerk cut me off."

As if giving that some thought, she ran a hand through her hair. "There's no hope for you, Kevin? You can't be trusted."

He noticed she wore jeans and a white blouse,

looking casually hot, even while she belittled him. Damn. He wished she'd come home.

"I bet you stopped off at Rory Dolan's for a pint and got caught up with one of the regulars, old Don Berger is my guess. You shouldn't be hanging out with him. He's a bad influence—"

"Corin..." Kevin frowned. "No way. I came straight home. Frank made me work overtime, the prick. You know I wouldn't miss this game for anything." He looked over her shoulder. "Where's Ethan?"

"Upstairs. He's been asking when his dad is coming for the game."

"I know. I'm sorry. Tell him I'm here now." He reached for her hand.

She pulled away. "Don't touch me."

"Corin, how long are you going to keep this up? It's been six weeks."

Her brows furrowed. "We're not living with a drunk, Kevin. Did you sign up for AA like you promised?"

He looked at the floor. "I'm on the wagon. Isn't that enough?"

"No." She shook her head. "It's important for

you to stand up in front of a group of people and admit you have a problem. You'll develop a support system and help each other stay out of the bottle."

"I'm not going to air my dirty laundry in front of a bunch of strangers. Putting this family back together will be a big help."

"Help yourself first, then we'll think about coming home."

"You know I love you."

"This is not about love."

He swallowed hard. "Then you still love me?"

Ethan bounded down the stairs. "Dad, what took you so long?" He brimmed with an eight-year-old's enthusiasm. Ready to go, he wore a Yankee's t-shirt, shorts, and sneakers, but his black hair was an uncombed mop sticking out from under his NY cap. "We're still going to the game, right?"

Kevin got down on one knee. "Absolutely, kiddo. Ready to watch The Judge jack one out of the park?"

"Can I have a hot dog too?"

"You bet."

Ethan slapped Kevin with a high-five. "Let's go."

Kevin stood. "We're outta here."

Corin handed him two fresh masks. "You stay safe, wear your masks, and keep an eye on the alerts."

"We will. Thanks for the masks."

"Just in case." She exhaled. "If the alert level changes or you don't feel comfortable in the crowd, get out of there."

"I understand. Thanks."

"And Kevin...no drinking."

He held up his hands. "Yeah. Got it. Geeze. I told you I'm on the wagon."

Chapter Nine

Saturday evening, after sunset, Yankee Stadium buzzed with excitement as fans crowded the entrance. Kevin gripped his eight-year-old son's hand and fought through the throng. So far, there'd been no alerts in this area, and most fans didn't wear masks.

Ethan gripped Kevin's hand. He carried his mitt under his arm, and his black hair stuck out the sides of his Yankees hat. "Come on, Dad. The Judge is up to bat soon."

"I'm trying, buddy. Full house tonight."

"Should we be wearing our masks?"

Kevin kneeled and placed his hands on Ethan's shoulders. "You're safe with me."

"But the TV said the vampire virus is everywhere."

"Vampire virus? More hype than fact. Don't believe everything you hear on TV."

"But Mom told us to wear our masks."

"Of course she did. Mom's worry. That's what they do."

"I love you, Dad."

Sunshine flooded his soul. He hugged him. "Love you too, buddy. Let's go watch some baseball."

"All right."

They pressed through the turnstiles and walked into an immense hallway with a vast array of portraits on the high walls: Ruth, Gehrig, DiMaggio, Mantle, and other great Yankees. The aromas of grilled hot dogs, cotton candy, and fried chicken swirled in the air. Beyond the mezzanine, raucous fans clapped and chanted under the bright ball field lights: "Let's go Yankees. Let's go Yankees." On the one-hundred-foot centerfield screen, an enthusiastic Yankees cartoon-character fan cupped his hands behind his enormous ears while big bold letters jumped out: "I CAN'T HEAR YOU!"

"Let's go Yankees. Let's go Yankees."

Organ music blared. The stadium was a rockin'.

Getting closer to their left-field seats, Kevin

kept his eyes peeled for a beer vendor. What was a ball game without a couple of beers?

Where is that damn guy?

Kevin stopped at a booth where they were selling Don Mattingly autographed Louisville Slugger bats. "I have to get one of these."

Ethan looked up at Kevin as fans pressed around them.

"Is Mattingly your favorite player?"

"Just like The Judge is yours."

With the bat in one hand and Ethan's hand in the other, Kevin found their seats overlooking left field. Even from here he could smell freshly cut grass. The fans seated in the row in front of them were boisterous and jumping up and down.

Kevin and Ethan stood so they too could view the ballpark.

A burly fan with a beer belly seated in the row behind them shouted, "Down in front."

They dropped down in their seats. Ethan's head was on a swivel. His eyes were wide with wonder. "Thanks for taking me here. This place is so cool."

Kevin smiled. "Only the best for my boy. My

dad took me here when I was eight, back in 1988. Mattingly hit a blast into the right field upper deck. I'll never forget it. They didn't call him Donnie Baseball for nothing." He held up the autographed bat as evidence.

Ethan's eyebrows rose. "Wow, that's awesome."

Kevin laid the bat at his feet. "I wish I was eight years old again."

"We'd be best friends."

"You think so, son?"

"I know so."

Over the loudspeakers, the announcer said, "Now batting Number 25."

Ethan tugged on Kevin's shirt. "Look, Dad." He jumped up, arms flailing. "Look who's in the on-deck circle. The Judge. Isn't he the best?"

"They pay him enough. He should be."

The prodigious righty took a couple of practice swings. Ethan jumped up and down. "Yea, Judge. Yea, Judge."

"Down in front."

"Take it easy, son. Be thoughtful of those seated behind you."

Jim Keane

Ethan sat down but had to lean and stretch to see around the fans standing in front of them.

A ruddy-faced beer vendor dressed in a blue pinstripe shirt and a backwards cap trudged up the aisle, lugging a metal box of iced-down beers. A circular metal pin on his shirt read: $12.50. "Beer here. Get your beer here. Bud Light. Heineken. Coors Light. Ice-cold beer. Get your beer here."

Kevin's hand shot up. *It's about damn time.* "Over here. Two Bud Lights." His mouth watered and his breath quickened.

The beer vendor nodded and lowered the beer carrier to the ground. "You got it, boss."

Ethan tugged on Kevin's shirt. "Dad, Mom told you no drinking."

"I'll be fine. Your mom worries too much." He handed three tens to the vendor. "Keep the change."

"Thanks, chief." He cracked open two twenty-four-ounce cans and passed them to Kevin. Foam oozed over the rim and cascaded down the side.

Kevin gulped from one of the cans, spilling foam on his jeans. Sure. He was supposed to be on the wagon, but ballgames didn't count.

Ethan frowned. "Mom is going to be mad."

"What she doesn't know won't make her mad." He chugged more beer.

"Are you going to get drunk?"

"Of course not. We're at the Yankees game, your first Yankees game, so we have to celebrate."

"I want a hot dog."

"I'm sure the hot dog guy will be around soon. Keep an eye out for him."

The crowd cheered. Number 25 had belted a screaming line drive into center field. At full speed, he rounded first base, digging up turf, but he stopped short as the centerfielder threw to second base. The crowd was on their feet as he scrambled back to the safety of first base, just before the ball slapped into the first-baseman's mitt.

"That was close," the announcer announced.

Amid Yankee fans' cheers and Red Sox fans' boos, The Judge strode toward the batter's box at home plate. The announcer's voice boomed over the loudspeakers. "All rise. Now batting, The Judge. Number ninety-nine."

Ethan shot up from his seat and pumped his

fist. "Yea, Judge. Jack one out of the park."

"Down in front, kid."

Kevin had half a notion to turn around and slap the crap out of the guy for bullying his son, but that was the nature of baseball. There was always a jerk in the stands, just like at work... A sudden and acidy burn rose in his chest. He guzzled more beer from the first can.

Trumpets blared. The one-hundred-foot screen flashed a message: *VIRUS ALERT - RISK LEVEL – MEDIUM. PUT ON YOUR MASKS.*

Kevin's stomach rolled. More fans than not were now wearing their masks.

Ethan tugged on Kevin's shirt. "We need to put on our masks."

"Watch the game. Here comes The Judge."

The fans chanted, "MVP, MVP, MVP."

Kevin turned around. The burly bully had his mask on, as well as the fans around him. For Kevin to put a mask on now, and help Ethan with his, he'd have to put down the beer cans and risk them getting kicked over and spilled. As he weighed this dilemma, the crowd went crazy as The Judge set his stance for the first pitch. It came in bullet-fast.

"Strike One," the ump called out.

The crowd grumbled.

Ethan cupped his hands around his mouth. "Come on, Judge. You can do it. Blast one out of the park."

The next pitch went wide-left.

"Ball."

"They're gonna walk him," Ethan shouted. "That's not fair."

"Down in front, kid."

Ethan paid the bully no mind.

The windup, the pitch. CRACK. The Judge blasted a rocket toward the left field bleachers. The crowd-noise exploded into a cacophony of exaltation, madness, and gratitude for The Judge.

The ball arced toward Kevin. He froze, stomach-churning, and gripped the beer cans. He'd forever dreamed of a moment like this...the ball kept coming.

"Dad. It's coming right for you. Drop the beer and catch it."

That moment of indecision proved costly.

Ethan held his mitt above Kevin's head. "I got

it." The spiraling ball sailed toward his mitt. "I got it."

Kevin ducked, sloshing beer on the ground.

The bully's hairy-knuckled hand shoved Ethan's mitt aside and caught the ball, snatched from the kid as any bully would do. He pumped his fist-full-of-baseball in the air. "Yeah. I'm the man." He high-fived the fans around him.

Ethan slumped down in his chair. "I almost had it, dad...but you could've caught it. All you had to do was drop the beer...now look." He glared at the celebrating bully behind them.

Kevin gazed around, half in shock, it had happened so fast. The bully's smile was evident, even behind his black mask. His reflexes were quick, and he got the prize, and Kevin knew he had disappointed his son. He let his gaze sink to the ground and saw scraps of popcorn, peanuts, and cracker jacks scattered about, just where he belonged, in the gutter with the garbage and trash. "I'm sorry, son," he muttered. "I was afraid to spill my beer."

Ethan shook his head. "What's wrong with you?"

Kevin slumped into his seat and dropped the beers on the ground. "Your mother was right. I shouldn't drink." He buried his face in his hands. *You can't help yourself. Nice going. You ruined the game for Ethan.*

Trumpets sounded. Ethan was hitting him on the shoulder. "Dad. Dad. Look."

The giant screen flashed a message. VIRUS ALERT - RISK LEVEL – HIGH! EVACUATE THE STADIUM.

His heart rate quickened. *Masks. We need our masks.*

Mayhem broke out behind him, cursing and scuffling. He turned to see the bully pummeling the man next to him, the same man he'd high-fived earlier, like they were best of buds. His eye sockets were ringed in black and spittle flew out of his now maskless mouth. "Nobody's taking my ball. I caught it. Not you. You'll have to kill me first."

"What? Are you crazy? I don't want your damn ball."

"I'll kill you..."

The men around him tried to restrain him, only

to be tossed aside like they weighed nothing. They tumbled down the bleachers, crashing into fans, who turned to attack him with needle-like teeth and snapping jaws.

Ethan clutched Kevin's arm. "Dad... I'm scared."

Kevin took two masks from his pocket. "Here, put this on."

"Are we going to die?"

"Not if I can help it." Kevin put on his mask and picked up the baseball bat at his feet. "Now stay close to me."

The black-eyed bully grabbed up a fan who'd jumped into the fray to help restrain him, then bit him in the neck with such ferocity that blood spurted from the jugular and splattered everyone around. As the bully sucked and swallowed copious amounts of blood, the grossness caused everyone else to back off. Then one by one they began to attack each other.

Kevin's heart thwacked against his ribs as he led his son, bobbing and weaving, through the mania Yankee Stadium had become. Fans attacked fans. Blood spurted. Howls and screams replaced the cheers and fanfare. The same scene repeated itself everywhere in the stands, and down on the field. The players raced into the dugouts where their individual fates would not be witnessed.

"Dad, what's happening?"

Kevin shouted over his shoulder to Ethan. "The virus is out of control. Stay close to me."

"I'm scared."

"Me too. Just keep moving. We're going home."

"But how, Dad? With all these crazy people."

"I'll protect you." He swung the bat at an attacker and pressed forward. His shoes lost traction on the blood-soaked concrete aisle and he damn near fell.

"Watch out, Dad."

A maniac ripped out the throat of his victim, and blood dripping from his maw, he stabbed a bloody finger at Kevin. "Give me the bat." His black-rimmed eyes bulged with madness.

Kevin raised the bat. "Get away from us."

The bloody man lunged at him, howling like a banshee. Kevin swung like The Judge and cracked the maniac upside the head, knocking him back into the seats where two men jumped on him and started tearing him to pieces.

Kevin snatched up Ethan in his arms. "Hold on tight."

"Stop, Dad. I dropped my mitt."

"I'll get you another one."

"I want my mom."

"Me too." Kevin pushed through the crowd with Ethan's arms wrapped around his neck. He swung the bat wildly at anyone who came at them, including the beer vendor who appeared to have developed a taste for blood. The bat connected with his forehead. Beer cans and ice went flying.

Ethan sobbed and gripped Kevin tighter. "I don't want to die."

"Keep your head down and close your eyes." *No child should ever have to see such bloodshed.*

The hallway of Yankee portraits was now a temple of mayhem. Fans rushed every-which-way, some screaming bloody murder as they chased down the uninfected, trying to flee. Slipping in blood and gore, Kevin dodged the maniacs and whacked others with the bat until he finally broke through the turnstiles and made it to the street. In every direction he looked, the infected were feeding on fallen fans. A minefield of gore lay between him and his parked car.

Ethan cried, "We're not going to make it."

Chapter Ten

At her parents' house in Mystic Estates, Corin planted her trembling hands on her cheeks and witnessed the pandemonium and massacre unfolding on television. All hell had broken loose at Yankee Stadium.

BREAKING NEWS. CDC ALERT IS UPGRADED TO EXTREME. STAY INDOORS. KEEP AWAY FROM THE INFECTED. At the bottom of the screen, a scrolling banner read: CHAOS ENSUES WHILE MUTATED FANS RAMPAGE THROUGH YANKEE STADIUM.

The carnage on-screen was not suitable for some viewers. Corin couldn't breathe. The living room seemed to spin. Nausea bubbled in her throat as her heart clobbered against her chest walls.

A somber-looking anchor wearing a black shirt and tan jacket reported the news.

After Sunset

"This is Andrea O'Shea from the CNN News desk. We're reporting live from Yankees stadium via a helicopter because it is too dangerous to get a reporter on the ground. I have to warn you, viewer discretion is advised."

River Avenue and Jerome Avenue were filled with Police Cars. Helmeted cops in full police riot gear held German shepherds on leashes.

Kevin and Ethan are out there. Oh my God, my boy.

A chill gripped Corin's spine.

What was I thinking, letting Kevin take Ethan to the Yankees game? Oh, my little boy. God damn, I'm an idiot.

She clenched her fists and called Kevin's cell phone, got a fast busy tone. Several more tries came with the same result. She could only hope he was sober enough to survive.

She always had known Kevin was a party boy, but he was always a fun drunk, never a barf-behind-the-dumpster drunkard. After getting married, he'd settled down some, changed his priorities, and after Ethan showed up, he didn't have time to go out drinking. But after years of working at Vericom, he changed, hit the bar after work, got sloppy drunk, belligerent to the point of abusive. Landed in the slammer for drunk and disorderly. Oh, he was always sorry, but he didn't change, wouldn't change.

I was right to move out of the house.

Her parents stood near her with their arms wrapped around each other, watching the television horror show. Then, with his glasses on the crook of his nose, her grey-haired father had to say something stupid and unhelpful. "Corin, I can't believe you agreed to let Kevin take our grandson to the game. What were you thinking?"

Then her mother, wearing an Irish sweater with her white hair resting on her shoulders, chimed in. "We never liked Kevin anyway."

Corin felt her cheeks redden. "This isn't his fault. He'll get Ethan home safely."

Her mother scowled. "Marrying that fool. You're a disappointment to this family."

Her father jumped in. "You're unfit to be a mother."

Are those black circles around his eyes?

"Dad? Mom? What's wrong with you?"

Her father stabbed a finger at her. "What are you going to do about him?"

"He's probably on his way home now."

"What if he's not?"

"I don't know."

"You better go look for him," Dad growled out.

Jesus Christ, Ethan could be ripped to shreds as they speak. Oh my God, what am I going to do?

"It's total anarchy at Yankees stadium," Andrea O'Shea said from the TV. "And it's a bloodbath on the corner of River and Jerome. People are attacking each other with no regard for civility...no regard for humanity. It's complete chaos. I've never seen anything like this. Hundreds are dead. The NYPD is overwhelmed. Brave police officers don't stand a chance, even with their riot gear. Some are shooting live rounds into the crowd." She hesitated with a finger on her earpiece. "We're just getting word that the National Guard has been dispatched to the scene."

A fist pounded on the door.

Dear God, let that be Ethan and Kevin. What if it's the police? What if Kevin and Ethan are dead? She shuddered and hurried to the door, heart hammering. When she opened the door, Kevin rushed inside with Ethan. She dropped to her knees and hugged him. "Thank God."

Kevin held up a bloody baseball bat. "I got him home, safe like I said I would." He turned and locked the door. His eyes were wide, and his breathing was rapid. "That was close."

Corin wasn't listening. She was doting over Ethan. "My boy, are you all right. Let me look at you. I saw the news reports."

Ethan sobbed. "Dad saved me."

Corin glared at Kevin. "This is all your fault. You shouldn't have taken him there."

Kevin buried his fingers in his hair. "You said it was alright. How were we supposed to know that everything would go crazy?"

Corin's parents stormed to Kevin. Both of their eyes were encircled by black, decaying skin. Her father shook a fist at him. "You piece of shit. You almost got my grandson killed. I ought to put you out of your misery." He bared his teeth. Normally, he was a pretty mellow guy, but now he was in a rage.

And as for Corin's mother, ugly veins pulsed in her neck under skin so pale, Kevin thought surely she must've been dead. "You're a loser, Kevin. A drunk and a bad father. Not sure what my daughter ever saw in you. She must have felt pity for you. Why don't you go someplace and kill yourself?"

Corin's father laughed. "Yes, that's a good idea. How about in a garbage pit where you belong. We'd love to help you." He grinned wickedly, revealing pointy teeth and slime.

"Mom, Dad, why are you being so mean?"

Kevin backed away from Corin's parents. "Ethan...go upstairs and make it quick." He gripped the bat tighter.

"But Dad."

"Just go." He turned to Corin's parents. "Keep away from me." He edged closer to Corin and whispered to her. "They got the virus. I saw the same thing happen to people at Yankees stadium."

"You've been drinking, Kevin. I smell beer on your breath."

"Never mind that. You're not safe here. We need to get back to our house."

"Forget it, Kevin. They're just worried about Ethan."

Corin's parents snickered and stepped closer.

"Corin. I'm not kidding." Kevin raised the bat against her parents. "We've gotta go now."

Corin clenched her fists. "No. You've got to go now, Kevin. Threatening my parents like that. I never want to see you again."

"Look at them, Corin. All the mutants at Yankee Stadium had the same look."

"They're just tired from worry."

"They're going to kill you and Ethan."

"Now you're being ridiculous...just to cover for betraying us again. Go back to Rory Dolan's where you belong."

Kevin shook his head. "You don't know what you're talking about. Come back home with me...before it's too late."

Ethan ran down the stairs. "Mom. If Dad says go, we should go."

"Get back upstairs."

"But, Mom. Grandma and grandpa look weird."

Corin hugged Ethan. "No, baby. They're fine.

We're staying here."

Her parents snorted at each other.

"Corin, I'm begging you. Please. Let's get out of here before your parents attack us."

"Mom. Dad. Are you going to attack us?"

They snorted at her.

Ethan's eyes welled. "Mom, I'm scared."

Corin patted his head. "Baby, this is the safest place for us now."

Kevin grabbed her arm. "We're leaving right now."

Her dad lunged at Kevin.

He swung the bat, connected with the side of her dad's head, cocked it sideways, but his expression didn't change. He didn't even blink, but it stopped him cold.

Corin opened the front door. "Leave, Kevin. You've done enough damage to this family. Don't make me kill you."

"Corin?" Dark circles were starting to show around her eyes. "No shit." He stepped toward the door and motioned to Ethan. "Come on, son."

She grabbed him. "He's not going anywhere with you." Then the unthinkable happened. She sunk her teeth into his shoulder.

"Dad," he screamed.

"Ethan." But he knew the damage was done, and it could never be undone. "God damnit, Corin."

Her mom rushed him with clawed fingers extended.

Kevin had just enough time to duck out the door and slam it in her face. As he ran to the car, he heard the door splinter, looked back and saw the four of them staggering toward him. "Son of a bitch." Any hope of getting his family back had been totally erased from the realm of possibility. The loss tore out his heart, and for the briefest of moments he thought to stop running, turn around, and accept their same fate. Put an end to all the horror, the drinking, Frank Cicero, traffic jams, and even Marge the temptress. Embrace death or the new reality of a mutant, but one thing stopped him. The thought of never taking another drink, drove him to run, run like he'd never ran before. He'd get the car later. For now, the want of another drink, another glass of Beam, kept his feet moving all the way home.

Chapter Eleven

Kevin slammed the door behind him and hurled the bat on the floor. "God dammit, Corin. Why didn't you listen to me?" He massaged his temples. A headache burgeoned behind his right eye. *God, I could go for a drink right now.* He stormed to the kitchen and flung open the top cabinet where he stashed his liquor supply. Jim Beam and Johnnie Walker made his pulse race. As he reached for a bottle of sunshine, his conscience spoke up.

"Don't do it, Kevin. Your family needs you."

"Shut up. Corin left me, took my son."

"Drinking isn't the answer."

"What do you know?"

"I know what it did to your family. It's in the toilet, thanks to you and your drinking."

"Shit."

He banged the cabinet door shut and stalked to

the couch, pissed off for talking himself out of a drink. After clicking the television on, he slumped back and stewed.

BREAKING NEWS! THE RAGE VIRUS ALERT IS AT LEVEL EXTREME. STAY INSIDE.

"Bullshit." Staying inside hadn't saved Corin and Ethan.

A redheaded, blue-eyed news anchor, Jennifer McNulty, wearing a blue blouse and grey skirt sat at one side of a round table. New York City's skyline stretched across the background, obviously superimposed on a green screen. "Our next guest is infectious disease expert Doctor James Salkland from the Salkland Infectious Disease Laboratories in Yonkers."

A bespectacled, white-haired man in a dark suit and red tie sat across from her. He nodded to the camera.

"He's here to shed some light on, and possibly some hope for a vaccine or cure for this horrible pandemic that's spreading across the country. Doctor, thanks for coming on the show. I know you're busy."

"No problem, Jennifer. Glad to be here. These

are unprecedented times."

Kevin turned up the volume and leaned forward.

"What can you tell us about this Rage virus? It appears to be spreading south toward the city. How dangerous is this to New Yorkers?"

"We should all be alarmed and take precautions." Salkland steepled his fingers. "This is a highly contagious virus for which there is currently no vaccine. It attacks the brain's limbic system, which controls anger and aggression impulses, leaving the infected with no qualms against murder and cannibalism."

"Where could such a virus have come from?"

"Outer space, for all we know. I've never seen anything like it, possibly a bat virus, maybe from a Central American species Desmodus Rotundus."

"Vampire bats?"

"It's only speculation at this point."

"Does masking and social distancing keep the Rage virus from spreading?"

"It's not a respiratory virus, but the CDC recommends wearing masks and keeping a safe distance from others, six feet minimum. It's a better defense than nothing. If you must go outside after sunset, which I don't recommend, I would wear two masks, a face shield, rubber gloves, and a hazmat suit."

"After sunset?"

"There's been no incidents of attacks during daylight hours. Life appears to go on as normal until the sun goes down."

"It's truly a super-virus. Is everyone susceptible to it?"

"We don't know for sure, but generally, four-percent of the population is immune to one virus or another. Genetics may be a reason, or prior exposure to a novel virus through any number of environmental sources. Our tests are still in the early stages."

"While you're unsure of its source, shouldn't the government shut everything down until you know the cause?"

"I agree with a complete quarantine, but there are those higher-ups who don't believe the virus is that big of a threat. They think it'll run its course in two weeks. We in the scientific community believe that prognosis is both reckless and dangerous."

Kevin agreed. He'd witnessed the mutants' attack in Yankee Stadium, how the place went from baseball to chaos within minutes. No doubt about it, the virus was a lethal threat to everyone and wouldn't go away easily.

Jennifer asked, "What progress are you making on the vaccine?"

"We've developed a trial serum that shows some promise, however, the FDA requires irrefutable proof of efficacy, which requires months of test data. Meanwhile, vials sit in our cabinets while people die. The bureaucracy is unforgivable."

That hit Kevin hard. Corin and Ethan were suffering while vials of serum sat on shelves...untested and unapproved. Maybe he could convince the doctor to let him have a couple doses, for Corin and Ethan, volunteer them as test subjects. People did that all the time, risk their lives to test a new drug, a new cure. What did they have to lose? The least he could do was ask, and the worst that could happen, Salkland could tell him no.

Jennifer leaned forward. "Doctor, what can we do to save ourselves?"

"Fire," he said with a deadpan expression.

Jennifer gasped. "Burn the mutants?"

"Set them on fire, anyone exhibiting blackened skin around the eye sockets. Fire is the only way to stop them."

"You're suggesting people burn their wives, husbands, children...their loved ones if they even look like a mutant? Isn't that a bit barbaric?"

"Douse them with gasoline and burn them in the streets. Let the government come around and collect the charred remains for proper disposal."

"Are we headed back to the dark ages?"

"I agree it's abhorrent, but we don't fully comprehend the Rage virus's power. For sure, mutants are killing machines. They can't be bargained with. They can't be reasoned with. And they won't stop until every person on this planet is dead or one of them."

Jennifer's eyes were wide with terror. "There must be another way to stop them."

Dr. Salkland looked directly at the camera. "Until science develops a vaccine, self-defense is your only option against the mutants. They can transfer the Rage virus to you with one bite, one scratch. Stay clear of them. Barricade yourselves in your homes at night. Don't let them fool you. They are intelligent. They are clever. And they are persistent. Imagine humanity stripped of all inhibitions, empathy, and conscience. You are their enemy, all of you...all of us. They want your flesh and blood. Some of you will survive. Most will not." He turned his attention back to Jennifer. "Thank you for inviting me on your show. I must be going now. There is much to do before the end of the world."

The camera focused on Jennifer. She looked terrified. "Thank you for your insight into the Rage virus pandemic, doctor. I...we... Everyone... We wish you luck and God's speed finding a vaccine and a cure."

Electronic intro music came on, and *Breaking News* flashed on the screen.

"Up next...an update on the mayhem and murder at Yankee Stadium, after a short break."

The program went to commercial. Kevin turned off the TV. He had work to do, board up the windows, deadbolt the doors...

...a clicking noise...

From where? He listened intently, heard the clicking again. A lump formed in his throat. Were the mutants outside? Were they trying to get in? He picked up his trusty bat, and gripping it firmly, he followed the sound into the kitchen, to the patio door. Dizzy with fright, he approached the glass, bat raised, and spread the vertical blinds only enough to look out. City lights reflected off a low sky, heavy with tumultuous clouds. No black-eyed mutants, just Marge, her hair a raven cascade on her shoulders. "What the hell?"

He propped his bat against the counter, slid open the door a crack, and let in a cool spring breeze. "Marge, what are you doing out there? Haven't you seen the reports?"

"Thought you might need a little company." She held up two tumblers and a bottle of Smirnoff Blue Vodka. "If it's the end of the world, then I figured we should have a drink."

"I don't drink."

"You should."

He scanned the grassy shared backyard of their

luxury duplex, the row of trees along the fence-line. Most of his neighbors appeared to be home with lights on behind drawn curtains. No mutants in sight. "Go home, Marge."

She just stood there and stared at him. The look in her eyes reminded him of a homeless dog in one of those ASPCA commercials. "Maybe I'm scared, Kevin. Maybe I don't want to be alone tonight." She sobbed. "You can't send me away...you just can't." A sniffle.

"Okay. Okay. Enough with the waterworks." He slid the door open farther and let her in.

She set the tumblers on the counter and poured two fingers of vodka into each glass.

Kevin imagined mixing the vodka with cranberry-orange juice, or grapefruit with a couple of ice cubes and gulping it down. Beckoning vapors from the vodka crept into his nose. His throat dried.

Vodka shooters. Vodka and Tonic. Screwdrivers. Moscow Mules. Vodka sours. Hell, I would jump into an Olympic-sized pool of vodka right now. God, it would be glorious. I'd never be thirsty again.

Marge broke Kevin out of his trance. "They

look good, don't they?"

"They sure do, but..."

"If there was ever a time for a drink..."

"It's not a good idea."

"Just one drink."

One drink is how I get into trouble. That's how it always starts. Can't fall for the same trap again. I have to be sharp. Get ready for the mutants. "I can't."

"You wouldn't make a girl drink alone, would you?"

"There are dating websites where you're sure to find a new drinking buddy."

"But I want you." Vodka glass in hand, she leaned into him and parted her lips. "Nobody has to know, Kevin. It'll be our secret. You know, friends with benefits." She downed the glass of vodka as if it were lowly beer.

A blend of soft florals from Marge's perfume made her offer more inviting. Invisible fingers of guilt raked down his spine. He thought he'd never cheat on Corin, even if Marge was the last woman on earth... But something about her nearness, her openness, her willingness... her charms were biologically impossible to resist. As heat swelled inside, he considered her lips so close, the heat of her breath on his mouth, the want in her big brown eyes, and he gave in, pulled her body tight against his need, and gave her what she wanted.

When was a kiss not just a kiss? When it's delivered with wanton abandon. When it's lustful and not loving. When it's taboo. Then it became something animalistic, with the tongue sucking, and lip licking and deep breathing, the squirming and the shivers and the pawing. It felt so right. It felt so wrong, her tongue alien to him, so thick and forceful compared to Corin...

The phone rang. It was Corin's ringtone. What could she be calling about...after what had just happened? He pulled away, shattering the moment that should have never been. "Really, Marge." He inhaled. "We need to chill."

"And here we were doing so well." She picked up the glass she'd poured for him and slammed it back.

"I need to take this call. You need to go."

"Here I am, throwing myself at you, and you've gotta be an ass. It's the end of the world, goddamn it. You might not see the sunrise."

"I'll survive."

"Maybe I won't. Maybe I don't want to die alone."

Here come the tears.

"Marge. That's enough." He slid open the patio door. "Just go home."

"I'll leave my door open just in case you want to take up where we left off." And she was gone.

He slid the door closed, took a calming breath then answered the phone. "Hello, Corin." His tone was guarded, not knowing what to expect.

"Hey, sexy, what are you doing?"

"Your voice...you sound different."

"Guess what I'm wearing."

"What?"

"Your favorite pink negligee."

"Why?"

"Do you remember when you proposed to me and we made love. I want to recreate that moment."

"Corin, I'm confused. When we last spoke... you wanted to kill me. What's changed in the last hour?"

"Questions. Questions. What's with all the

questions?"

"I'm worried about you guys." He couldn't trust her. She probably wasn't even home, maybe outside his door. He decided to see for himself, grabbed the bat, and peeked out the patio door. Nobody was in sight. He stepped out, closed the door, and stalked around front. No one there, either. The moon shone down like a skull. He headed toward Corin's place.

"Kevin? Are you there?"

"I'm getting ready for bed. How about you and Ethan?"

"We're fine."

He hurried past houses on his left, sticking to the shadows in the community's shared backyards. Most of his neighbors appeared to be home.

"Kevin, where are you? It sounds like you're running."

"Just tired, is all. I've had a rough night." He was nearing Corin's parents' house. From here he could see the front curtains were partially parted, the window nestled behind a hedge of bushes.

"We're sorry you left in such a rush."

He snuck to the front of the house and crouched below the front window then scanned the area to be sure nobody else was about.

"I'd like to make it up to you."

"How's that?"

"I'm cooking a pot roast with potatoes, carrots and gravy. Come back and we'll have dinner together like a normal family."

He rose up and peered into the living room. She sat on the couch with Corin's parents and Ethan huddled around her. No sign of a pink nightgown. Their eyes were encircled by blackened, decaying skin, and their faces had turned ghastly pale. Corin's father clutched a knife. Her mother rubbed her hands together with malevolent glee. Even Ethan had changed into a monster, his hands like claws. His innocence had been ripped away by his own mother. Now they were ghouls, blood-lusting specters planning to kill him, lure him with pot roast to rip him to shreds, or perhaps, make him join their growing numbers.

Powerful dread squeezed his throat.

"Kevin? Can you still hear me, baby?"

"Yes. I'm thinking about that pot roast. Sounds delicious."

"And it smells divine. I miss you so much. Ethan misses you too." Corin gave the phone to Ethan. "Say hello to your dad."

Dad? Corin would never call him Dad.

"Hi, Daddy."

Daddy? Ethan always called him Dad. Kevin couldn't speak. His throat tightened. The voice of his deformed son had not changed, which made this charade even more horrible.

"Daddy, when are you coming over?"

A sickness filled Kevin's gut as he listened to the monster masquerading as his son. "Soon...I don't know."

"You okay, Daddy? You don't sound good."

"I'm...fine, son. Just a little sore throat."

"We can come over and make you feel better."

I'm sure you can.

They got up in unison and staggered toward the front door, a pack of ghouls making their way to the next grave. His grave.

A cold pulse oscillated down his spine. He willed his legs to move, but they were noodles.

Come on, Kevin. Get the hell out of here.

"No, Ethan. You stay there. I'll come over for dinner. See you in a few minutes."

"Okay, Daddy. We'll be waiting."

He watched them return to the couch then hung up the phone and bolted from the bushes, hoping that lie would buy him some time. When he was no longer within line of sight from the window, he sprinted toward his house.

Moments later and out of breath, he scrambled inside and locked all the doors and windows.

When they realize I lied about coming to dinner, they'll storm over here, and not for a social visit. I have work to do.

Inside the attached garage, he gathered lumber he had stashed for the fireplace, grabbed a box of nails and a hammer. Then, he went to work, boarding up the windows.

His phone rang. It was Corin. "What do you want, Corin?"

"I thought you were coming over."

"I had to board up my windows."

"You know, don't you."

"That there's no pink nightgown and pot

roast?" He envisioned Corin's deep-set eyes with black circles. "Easy to figure out you're trying to trick me. What are you going to do, Corin, kill me?"

"No. We can be a family again. I want you to join us."

"No you don't. I'm a drunk, remember?"

"Your drinking doesn't matter now. You don't know the power I'm feeling. It's incredible."

"I saw firsthand what that power can do at Yankee Stadium. People were slaughtered because of your kind."

"I can't protect you from the others, and they will come for you. Especially Frank Cicero. He wants you dead, so you need to join us to survive."

"Corin, listen. Scientists are working on a vaccine...a cure. One of them has a lab in Yonkers, not fifteen miles from here. I'll go see him, get the serum, even if it's experimental, and I'll bring it back for you and Ethan."

"I don't want a serum. And Ethan doesn't want it either. We feel great."

"You don't look great. Have you looked in a

mirror lately?"

"Think about it, Kevin. You won't last long without my help. Our numbers are growing by the hour."

"I'll find a way to save you."

An outburst of shouting outside froze him. He peeked out the front window and saw a mob of mutants approaching his townhouse. His heart lurched. It amazed him how fast they found him... Rocks slammed against the kitchen window, and fists pounded on the front door. It seemed like a coordinated attack.

"We know you're in there, Tippler." The guttural bellow of Frank Cicero came from outside his front door.

Blood boiled in Kevin's veins. *How can this get any worse?*

"Do something useful for once in your life and open this door."

"Go to hell, Frank," Kevin shouted through the door. "I'm off the clock."

"You're breathing up my air. You don't respect the company and you're too old to be working there."

"Sounds like the Rage virus has improved your disposition, Frank. You've never been so kind to me."

"You're fired, Tippler."

"What does it matter now? The world's coming to an end."

"It matters to me."

"Of course it does, Frank. You're a nice guy. Is there anyone left at Vericom?"

"Why do you care? You're fired."

"I'll be there on Monday."

"You won't live that long. There's too many of us now."

"Don't count on it, Frank. I got a baseball bat with your name on it."

Frank slammed against the door. The walls shook but the door held. "I'm right here, Tippler. Come out and give it your best shot."

White light exploded behind Kevin's eyes. He wanted to rip open his barricaded door and bash Frank's head in just to shut him up.

The mutants' howls and screams formed a hellish cacophony.

Kevin backed away from the door with his

hands clamped on his ears. The thrashing of his heart sent shock waves through his chest. It was six hours before dawn. He had to survive until then.

They pelted his house with rocks, sticks, and bricks and pounded on the door. Windows shattered, and the only thing keeping the bastards out were the boards he'd haphazardly nailed into place.

The mutants howled.

Sweat broke out on Kevin's face as he worked double-time to reinforce the boarded windows and doors before the mutants could break through his defenses and rip him limb from limb. There would be no sleep tonight. He could only hope to be lucky to survive long enough to see the sunlight again.

He back-stepped to a corner of the room, slumped to the floor, and pulled his knees to his chest to hug his legs. His breaths came in gasps, yet there wasn't enough air. The deeper he gasped, the more his thinking clouded. He gaped at the top cabinet where his glorious army stood at the ready: rum soldiers, bourbon sergeants, vodka lieutenants, and of course, General Jim Beam. How sweet it would be to call them to the front line, pour himself a tall glass of reinforcements on the rocks. Then another and another and let courage in a bottle lead him into battle with Frank Cicero, to victory, to freedom. Blitzed out of his mind, he wouldn't fear anything, feel any pain, all to save his family from the Rage virus. He would stand glorious before Corin and Ethan, serum in hand, and they would praise him as their savior and forgive him for his drinking problem. If all this was a fantasy, what would one drink matter anyway? Whatever he suffered after that drink settled deep, he wouldn't care in whiskey's soft embrace.

The howls of the mutants increased, and he forgot about alcohol winning his war against the mutants. Instead, he snatched up his bat, the Louisville Slugger signed by Don Mattingly, the bat he'd gotten at the Yankees game with his son. They'd had a good time before all hell broke loose. Now Mattingly was all he had left.

Window glass shattered. Wood splintered and clattered on the floor. He ran to the kitchen and gaped at a pasty hand that groped in between the remaining wood planks. If he didn't do something quick, the mutants would breach his defenses. He ran to the window, reared the bat, and slammed it on the intruding hand. It retracted, and its owner shrieked like a woman, and when he peeked out through the slats, he saw Marge Thompson, black-eyed and white as death, cradling her broken right arm.

Son of a bitch. It hurt his heart to see her lumbering about with the others as her hand flopped around, broken above the wrist. However, she'd taught him something valuable.

Mutants feel pain.

He set the bat aside then picked up the fallen wood slat. After hammering it back into place, Frank's hairy-knuckled finger poked in through a crack, so he nailed it with the hammer, and it pulled back out of view.

The house suddenly went dark. The power was out.

He gathered up candles from a kitchen drawer, set them about the house and lit them. One by one, as the darkness receded, he didn't feel any safer.

He found his flashlight, but the batteries were dead. He'd have to get more when he went out for supplies...if he lived until sunup. Then he'd stock up on canned goods, and damn how he missed the fish-and-chips platter at Rory Dolan's.

As the pounding worsened and the mutants screamed louder, Kevin retreated from the kitchen with the bat. It sounded as if there were a thousand mutants surrounding his house, an angry mob of doom. Where were the police, the National Guard, and the US Army?

He knew the mutants were smart enough to work together. They had the single-mindedness to kill for blood, flesh, and proliferation. However, he was still alive, like they were saving him for some special occasion. Or maybe he'd just been lucky. A preemptive strike might improve his odds. He should hunt them during the day, find their hiding places, set them on fire and cut their numbers. That sounded like a good plan. If he lived, he'd get supplies, come back, and reinforce the house. So many things to do, but he was exhausted. He needed to sleep, rest up for tomorrow's sorties.

After one last check on the window and door fortifications, he bolted up the stairs, taking two steps at a time, leaving the screams to echo around the townhouse below him.

He raced into the master bedroom, slammed the door, then drew the curtains. After lighting a candle, he set it on the nightstand.

In the walk-in closet, he lit another candle and set it on the dresser. A panel in the ceiling allowed access to the attic via a small ladder that pulled down. If the mutants got in, he could retreat to the attic, even though he'd be trapped. He had to risk it. He needed the sleep. After he collapsed on the carpeted floor, he looked at a picture of Ethan on his cell phone. Ethan's eyes bubbled with enthusiasm. Hot tears rolled down Kevin's cheeks because it reminded him of the innocent, fun-loving boy, not the mutant who was now his son. He rubbed his eyes.

His phone beeped, displaying the low-power icon. *Damn, what else could go wrong? There's no electric service to charge it.* He turned off the phone, hoping to save any battery strength he had left.

Chapter Twelve

K evin awoke with a dry mouth, and his stomach hurt from emptiness. If the mutants had broken in, they hadn't made it upstairs. A glance at his watch, an old wind-up Timex his father had given him, a Mickey Mouse keepsake, told him it was six o'clock.

He had a lot of work to do, getting food and supplies, reinforcing the house, and finding Dr. Salkland's lab. No time for sleeping in this Sunday morning.

He powered on his cell phone, hoping to call work and see if the on-duty tech could help him get a phone number for Dr. Salkland. Vericom had all the resources needed to survive an apocalypse, including two massive Kohler 4000-kilowatt generators in case of a power outage. However, his cell phone immediately turned off because of the low battery.

Shit.

His knees popped as he rose from the floor. His arms felt sore from hammering all those nails into the boards on his windows and doors.

He lumbered into the master bathroom. The mirror didn't tell any lies. He ran a hand through his hair and a 2-day growth of beard. His eyes were puffy. He splashed water on his face.

In the bedroom, he pushed open the curtains and saw it was a cloudy day.

Gripping the bat, he opened his bedroom door, preparing for the worst. No mutants. He stalked the hallway, checked the bathroom on his right and then the two bedrooms farther down. Ethan's room, with his little bed and a hippopotamus on the pillow, was untouched since the day he'd left with his mother. Dr. Seuss books they'd read together lined a shelf. A tear burned his eye for those good days gone by.

He hurried down the stairs. Everything was the same as he'd left it last night. In the kitchen, a peek through a crack between boards on the patio door told him no mutants were visible, meaning they were hiding or had reverted to more civilized activities than the savagery he'd witnessed last night.

The pantry was nearly bare: a bottle of water and a can of tuna. He could make it easy for the mutants if he just starved himself to death, but that wouldn't help him find Dr. Salkland and save his family.

First, however, he would need to find them, and if he did, they were more likely to kill him than let him get close enough to administer an injection that would cure them.

He gulped the water then opened the tuna. It made for a lousy breakfast, but he needed energy. He selected a kitchen knife from the top drawer, an eight-incher with a serrated blade, which he hoped would be sufficient for killing mutants. Dr. Salkland had said to douse them with gasoline and light them on fire, but Kevin wasn't about to lug gasoline around. A knife would have to suffice, and if not, he'd likely be killed if he were to come into close combat with a mutant.

He stuffed the knife in his knapsack and took hold of his baseball bat. In the garage, as he raised the door, a stiff wind slapped him in the face, and he wrinkled his nose at the putrid stench of half-eaten bodies that lay in the street and gutters. The mutants were nowhere to be seen. Why had they scattered? Where did they go?

There must have been some hierarchy within the mutants' ranks, but he didn't have time to follow this up. He planned to keep the house barricaded at night, get more materials to reinforce his home, search for Dr. Salkland and his lab, and get supplies, all before sunset. That was enough on his plate.

To his right, rising smoke from a torched duplex leaned with the wind. Several cars had crashed into each other, a tree, and the bushes along Pond View Lane. One lay on its roof, windows shattered, and others were tangled in a field of their own debris.

He saw that many of the townhomes on his block had broken doors and busted windows, as if they'd already been looted. No telling how much food he'd find in them, but checking was worth a try.

He wondered if Ethan or Corin were close enough to hear him if he called them, so he stepped out on the driveway. "Ethan," he shouted.

"Corin." There was no answer, only the howling wind. He thought to call out for Frank. The bastard was the first one banging on his door last night, so he was probably hiding in one of the townhouses nearby. He weighed his options: forage for food or fight Frank. The empty pantry took precedence. He'd hunt Frank some other time.

There was a drugstore in town, five minutes by car, where he could scrounge for food and supplies, but he'd left his car at Corin's, so he'd have to ride his mountain bike. If he had to prepare for the long haul of an apocalypse, he'd need a truck.

He closed the garage door, stuffed the butt of his bat in his knapsack, and strapped it on his back. Then, he jumped on his bike and rode toward Mystic Estates' front gate.

Along the way, he noticed many townhomes suffered the same damage as his, indicating the mutants had attacked his neighbors, as well. He decided to check for survivors, stopped, and pulled out his bat. At one open door, he followed a blood trail from the living room, into the kitchen, and upon seeing the carnage, his stomach churned. The mutants had beaten the young couple to death. They lay in a pool of co-mingled blood; some of their limbs were missing. His heart flailed in terror and he felt faint, as this could be his own fate.

He would've called 911 if his phone wasn't dead. The lack of first responders in the area, or sirens in the air, made him think emergency services might not be functioning anyway.

He pedaled to High Ridge Road and stopped at Corin's parents' townhouse. It hadn't sustained any damage from last night. Maybe mutants didn't attack other mutants. How did they differentiate between infected and not infected? By sight or smell?

If Ethan, Corin, and her parents were inside, perhaps he could reason with them during the daytime while they weren't bloodthirsty mutants. He hoped they would listen to reason and be willing to accept the cure, should Dr. Salkland develop a vaccine or serum that could change them back to normal.

He hid his bike in the bushes out front and

took out his baseball bat from the knapsack. Peeking through the windows provided no information on their whereabouts. He tried the front door. It was locked. The back door was also locked, so he smashed out one of the kitchen windows. He pushed away shards of glass with his bat and crawled in and landed on the kitchen counter. On the floor, his sneakers crunched through the glass. Aromas of pizza and popcorn drifted through the kitchen. No sign of any pot roast. He ventured into the living room.

"Corin? Ethan?"

Nobody answered.

His feet strode silently up the stairs, and he paused at the landing. Shadows loomed in the hallway before him. Three doors were closed. He squeezed the bat, approached the first door, and then gripped the handle. His chest heaved as he opened the door.

Other than a tussled bed and clothes scattered on the floor, nothing caught his attention.

He approached the next door in the hallway. A horrible thought invaded his mind. What if he found them all dead in the bed together? Would a foul stench slap him in the face as soon as he opened the door? What would be left for him to live for?

He felt his neck muscles tense up as he tried the handle. Locked. He pounded on the door. "Corin, Ethan. Are you in there?"

Nobody answered.

He kicked in the door.

Standing in the dimly lit bedroom, he noticed the bed had several lumps underneath the blanket. In the murkiness caused by the closed shades, it was hard to determine the shape of what was under it. He crept to the bed, ripped back the covers, and found pillows. On one pillow lay a note...addressed to him:

Don't bother looking for us, Kevin. You'll never find us. But we'll find you soon. Join us or die.

Dread shot chills up his spine.

He ran downstairs, opened the front door, ran from the house, and jumped on his bike. In spite of the shock and the threat, he had to stay focused. He couldn't dwell on the fear that Corin might be watching him, waiting for a chance to strike, bite him, or tear him limb from limb.

Supplies. Get supplies.

He peddled toward the main gate. The trip was an obstacle course as he weaved his bike around crashed cars, windblown trash, and dead bodies. Mutants were probably hiding in the nearby abandoned homes, maybe even Frank, but he had more important things to do now than seek out their hiding places and try to kill them by driving a knife into their hearts.

As he peddled like mad, plumes of smoke and embers coiled from a townhouse on his left. He inhaled the acrid air and shivered at the thought of burned bodies inside.

He turned north on Albany Post Road, weaving in and around abandoned cars. A plane soared over the Hudson toward New Jersey. Boats and barges drew white wakes on the water. Life must have been going on as usual for many people not yet infected by the virus.

There was no traffic on the normally jammed road into Croton, so he made good time riding the mile and a half journey to the drugstore on Maple Street. Abandoned cars littered the parking lot. He stashed his bike behind a dumpster; hopefully nobody would swipe it while he was in the store.

He glanced at his Mickey Mouse watch. It was four o'clock, which gave him more than three hours to get back home before the mutants came out of hiding after sunset.

Before entering the store, he searched the open cars for keys. Maybe one of them had a full tank, but he didn't have any luck.

Black clouds lumbered overhead as he kicked through broken glass in front of a shattered window, and he entered the store. The only light came through the window openings and peppered the place in shadows. Normally he'd see clerks at the counter and workers in the aisles, stocking shelves, but today, mutants and looters had ransacked the place. He hoped he'd find something left of value. "Is anyone here?"

No response.

A putrid reek lingered in the air, and a trail of gore and bloody footprints led to the backroom doorway. He hoped the mutants weren't hiding in there, waiting for another victim to happen by.

Merchant displays had been knocked over, and several aisles of books and cosmetics were ripped down. It looked as if a tornado had rolled through the store. He envisioned a horde of enraged mutants tearing the store apart in a manic frenzy.

He found a dented can of chicken noodle soup, a bag of peanuts, and a bottle of water, which he stuffed into his knapsack. Not a huge score, but it was something, as looters had pretty much picked the store clean. They'd missed a small flashlight lying on the floor. He picked it up and clicked it on. A bright halogen beam shot out.

In hopes of finding supplies and food not yet put out on the selves, he headed for the backroom. He pushed past tipped over shelving and stacks of upended chairs, which blocked part of the narrow aisle that led to the backroom. Finally, he reached the damaged door, leaning off its hinges: *EMPLOYEES ONLY*. It looked as if fists had pounded on the door, leaving bloody and smeared handprints.

Had the employees barricaded themselves in the backroom? A last stand against the mutants?

Panic sprinted through him. He took a deep breath and clenched the bat as he passed through the doorway.

Gagging, he covered his nose, as the stench was pungent in here. Bile climbed to the back of his throat. He clicked on the flashlight, and the beam illuminated an employee room doorway to which the bloody footprints had fled. Inside, there were a half-dozen lockers, a destroyed vending machine, and a shattered coffee pot. Blood had splattered and dripped down the walls.

He shined the light at a uniformed man slumped on the floor. A clump of meat was missing from his neck, and a river of blood had flowed from the carcass to the floor drain, the trail now congealed to black goo.

His shirt read: HEALTH IS EVERYTHING.

He hoped the man had died quickly.

These massacres are so brutal, so mindless.

As he searched the employees' break room for anything of value, he heard a groan come from inside a locker. It was much too narrow for someone to hide inside, but there it was again. A groan, for sure. The hair on his neck prickled. His first instinct was to beat feet out of there, but he had to know who was in that locker. Maybe someone needed help. He approached it with the bat at the ready, released the latch, and stepped back to see a man had squeezed himself into the tight confines.

"Please...don't...kill...me." His eyes were ringed in black decay, and his face was as pale as a white picket fence.

"You're a mutant. What are you doing in there?"

"Hiding."

"Why?"

"That's what mutants do."

"You forgot the part about eating human flesh."

"I get hungry...I get angry."

Kevin pointed to the dead man on the floor. "Did you kill that employee?"

The mutant grinned, showing off a thick row of pointy teeth. Worse, coagulating blood oozed from the corners of his mouth.

Kevin poked the bat at him. "Sounds like a good reason to kill you."

"Don't come near me."

There was something off about this guy. Seems he would have jumped out in a murderous frenzy, probably would have if it were after sunset, but then again, mutants were smart and cagey. He might be waiting for the right moment to pounce. Just to be on the safe side, Kevin slammed the locker door shut.

The sudden bang sent the mutant into a rage. Screaming like a banshee, he started pounding on the metal door, each blow bulging the steel outward and filling the room with the banging sounds of his madness. Any second now, he'd bust out.

Kevin stepped back and raised the bat like Mattingly at home plate, waiting for the pitch.

The locker door blew from its hinges, and the mutant leaped out at him, screaming, its clawed fingers outstretched with murderous intent.

If Kevin had a split second to think, he'd consider the ramifications of knocking this guy's head into left field, the damage it would cause to his skull, his brains, and the bloody mess that would splatter all over the walls. Would the blow kill him, Kevin didn't know, nor was he sure he had the mettle to kill any living soul, mutant or otherwise. He could only hope the bat would stop the mutant in mid-flight. Unfortunately, he didn't have time to think, just react. He swung the bat with all his might.

The crack of wood against bone echoed through the break room, rattling the other locker doors. Before the mutant hit the floor, the thunder of raging fists against metal rose to a deafening roar. The lockers were jerking and slamming about as the raging forces within tried to escape, and Kevin knew their anger would be immediately directed at him. It was time to blow this pop stand before he was served up as dinner to a flesh-hungry mob.

Outside, he jumped on his bike, and holding the bat and flashlight in one hand and steering with the other, he fast-pedaled across the parking lot. The daylight seemed to be fading, though he figured he had two hours of sunlight left. He rode toward a grocery store down the road where he hoped to find better pickings.

As he reached the top of the hill on Riverside and glanced down at the store's parking lot, he knew he'd made a mistake. A horde of mutants were milling around in front. He looked west and saw the sun had set on the New Jersey horizon.

Son of a bitch. How did I lose track of time?

He checked with Mickey Mouse again. It was still four o'clock. The second hand stood dead still. Damn. He'd forgotten to wind it. Now he was in deep do-do.

The horde of mutants spotted him and raced toward him, screaming obscenities and threats: "Fresh meat," and "Catch him," and "Kill him," and "I got dibs on his brains." Cold fear rushed through his veins. To his right, mutants charged out of a Vericom cell phone store. Rage made their ashen faces uglier than ever. He wheeled the bike around only to see the mutants from the drugstore running toward him. Leading the pack was the guy from the locker. The left side of his head was bashed in, the eyeball hanging by a thread, and his jaw was jacked over to the right. He looked mad enough to eat railroad spikes.

"Crap."

Kevin took a hard left and raced to the 9 ramp that would take him south toward home. His legs pumped the pedals, sweat broke out on his brow, and his frayed nerves felt like fire running down his spine. And if that wasn't bad enough, his brain came up with a terrible possibility.

What if Frank and Corin are waiting for me?

He looked back to see he'd left the gang of mutants far behind. After crossing over the Croton River bridge, the bike hit a pothole and bucked him off. He skidded across the pavement, collecting road rash on the palms of his hands. The bat and flashlight clattered into the gutter.

Enraged mutants poured from a church and raced toward him.

Get up, or you're dead.

He scrambled to his feet, recovered the bat and flashlight, jumped back on the bike and pedaled past a Crotonville industrial area on his left. Dozens of mutants funneled from businesses and warehouses and spilled onto the highway. Once they spotted him, they turned like a flock of birds and raced toward him, their clawed fingers swiping the air.

How am I going to get out of this mess?

The distraction caused him to sideswipe a retaining wall, but he regained his balance and kept his legs pumping. Only now did he wish he'd drank less and exercised more. The cushy sit-down job at Vericom had come back to haunt him, as well. His heart was a sledgehammer in his chest and his lungs were about to have a blowout. Finally, he crossed through the front gates into Mystic Estates and steered left toward his townhouse.

Twilight filled the sky. Every luxury duplex was dark, except for the ones on fire. Dogs roamed the streets, sniffing bodies and licking the bloody faces of their dead masters. Stopping at the corner on Pond View, he saw a horde milling about his front lawn and testing the strength of his windows. His blood ran cold and he swallowed hard. Frank Cicero led the pack. Kevin didn't want to risk confrontation to get inside his house, but he knew he couldn't get past them. That left only one option. Go around. By this time, the mutants had spotted him and started running in his direction, screaming and cursing.

He spun a one-eighty and pedaled like mad, back the way he came. The muscles in his legs started to cramp, but he pumped down the block of duplexes while screams and howls roared from the pack of mutants running behind him.

Someone crossed his peripheral vision, a woman running toward the clubhouse. Red hair, white t-shirt, jeans... Then she was gone. Didn't she know she wouldn't survive out here for long? He couldn't help her; he had his own troubles. She'd have to fend for herself.

He skidded the bike right and onto a walking path that took him through the trees and around to the back of his townhouse. His boarded windows had held, and there was no way in through the patio door, so he stalked around to the front, hoping all the mutants had left to chase after him. Seeing the coast was clear, he opened the garage door and hustled his bike inside, only to be attacked by a mutant that jumped from the shadows.

Marge Thompson knocked him down. "Hey, neighbor. Can I borrow some sugar?"

The bat rattled on the floor, and he groped for it, but she slammed him into his garbage cans. He winced, tried to get up, but Frank landed on top of him and groped for his throat.

"Welcome home, Tippler. We've been waiting

for you."

He recoiled from the disgusting stench spewing from Frank's mouth. Holding his breath, he got in a roundhouse punch to Frank's temple. It was enough force to knock him backwards, giving Kevin a second to grab the bat and swing it at Frank's head. *Crack.* Home run. He landed on his ass on the floor, his cheekbone caved in, and now he was seething mad. "I was going to kill you quickly, but now I'll make you suffer for a long time."

Marge made a one-armed lunge for Kevin's throat.

He showed her the fat end of the bat. "You want some of this too?"

She stepped back, and he noticed her broken arm no longer had a hand, as if she'd gnawed it off at the wrist, leaving two jagged pale bones protruding from the red meat of her forearm. At first, he felt sorry for breaking her arm with the bat, but she shouldn't have reached for him between the boards on his kitchen window.

Frank got to his feet and charged toward him.

Kevin swung the bat. Don Mattingly connected

with Frank's stomach, bowling him over. He rolled out of the garage and onto the driveway. More mutants with glaring eyes and bared teeth raced up to join the battle.

There are so many. I can't fight them all.

Kevin pulled on the rope to close the garage door, but a mutant's hand grabbed the bottom panel and flung the door up. Mutants poured in and cornered him. He swung the bat at his attackers, but they overpowered him, and the bat clattered to the floor.

The creatures dragged him out of the garage, and holding his arms, stood him up in front of Frank. The crazed mutant licked his chops like a dog at dinner time. "I've been looking forward to this." His rows of teeth dripped slobber, and a bit of his skull poked out of his left temple, thanks to Mattingly.

Kevin stood there, ready for the worst, to accept his death with open arms and a suitcase full of relief. It was finally over: the fear, the cowering, the running... "Give it your best shot, Frank."

Frank punched him in the gut, doubling him over in agony. As fire filled his belly, pain exploded in his head with blinding whiteness as Frank's fist came in with an uppercut. Kevin hung his head and watched blood from his lips drip on the driveway.

"There's nothing like fresh blood." Frank laughed.

The mutants howled in agreement.

Marge sauntered up to Kevin, lifted his chin with her only hand, and smirked. His eyes met her black-rimmed orbs, and he remembered the kiss, those beautiful lips now gnarled and oozing pus. "We could have had it all, Kevin, but now it's too late. You're going to die. What a shame." She dropped his chin, leaned into Frank, and pawed at his arm.

"Looks like you've got...Frank now." Kevin's breath came in spurts. "You deserve each other."

"You lose again, Tippler."

Howls from the mutants around him rose into the night sky.

I tried, Ethan and Corin. I hope I see you in Heaven some day. Dear God, make my death quick.

Tears streamed down his cheeks. He thought of Ethan, his eyes wide and a big smile on his face, an image he'd take with him into eternity.

Frank reached out and gripped Kevin's throat. "I'm so going to enjoy ripping out your—"

"Hey." A woman's voice stopped him.

Kevin craned his neck to see the redhead he'd seen earlier, running toward the clubhouse.

Frank glared at her and grunted. Saliva dripped from his ugly maw. "Get her."

She took off running.

Marge and the mutants ran after her, including the two ghouls who were holding his arms.

"No, wait," Frank shouted. "Get back here."

In that instant of distraction, Kevin struck Frank's forearm, knocking the hand from his throat, and he fled toward his open garage, but Frank regrouped quickly and tripped him.

Kevin crashed into his garbage cans, stumbled over his bike, hit the cement floor, and groaned.

"Where do you think you're going?" Frank kicked him in the ribs. "I'm not done with you."

His ribs burned, might even have been broken, but Kevin wouldn't give Frank the satisfaction of seeing him hurt. "Is that the best you can do?"

Frank doubled-down with a second kick, this

time to Kevin's stomach.

Despite the pain, Kevin struggled to his feet. "You'll have to do better than that."

Frank balled a fist and knocked him to the ground. "I can do this forever, Tippler." He grabbed him by the collar, and with vise-like fingers, lifted him back to his feet. "I'll never get tired of kicking your ass." He kicked him in the groin, and Kevin hit the floor again, this time of his own accord. By now the mutant mob had returned and gathered at the open garage door to watch the shit-show that would be his murder.

Did they kill that woman already? Did she get away?

Kevin, on his hands and knees and fighting that horrible gut-pain every man dreaded, crawled toward the bat on the floor. He clenched his jaw so tightly his teeth hurt, too.

And I thought dying would be easy.

Frank was right behind him. "In what world did you ever think you could beat me." His hot breath chilled the back of Kevin's neck.

He snatched up his bat, rolled on his back, swung, and smashed one of Frank's kneecaps.

His leg buckled, and as Frank bent over, Kevin delivered a Hail Mary blow to his head. It snapped back, and the mutant audience gasped and shuffled backwards as Frank's teeth flew through the air. Cupping his mouth, he staggered out of the garage, giving Kevin the precious seconds he needed to close the garage door.

The mob pounded on the door and screamed bloody murder.

Frank shouted, "You're a dead man, Tippler."

Kevin staggered back, eyes bleary, legs aching, mouth dry, and sweat raced down his face. His body was one massive cramp as the muscles tightened around his aching bones. However, he managed to drag the bat and knapsack into the kitchen.

Now the yapping cries and howls of the jackals closed in around the house. Frank growled at the front door. "Why are you wasting your time? You'll never stop us. Just give up."

There were more mutants than he had thought possible. Even if he could systematically kill them, the task would be like chipping away an iceberg with a spoon. He dropped the bat and his knapsack on the kitchen counter.

Frank continued his verbal assault. "All you have to do is open the door, and we'll do the rest. Can't you see resisting is futile? We can hunt you forever."

"Shut up," Kevin shouted with his fists clenched. He couldn't give up. Dr. Salkland might discover a vaccine to help eliminate this plague and cure the mutants. There was still hope that he could return to his everyday life, working at Vericom and coming home each night to his loving family.

Where there's hope, there's a reason to live.

"Come outside, Tippler." Frank pounded on the front door.

Kevin collapsed on the kitchen floor and covered his face with his trembling hands.

The world is going to Hell, and all I want is a drink.

"You can't win."

What if there are no other survivors?

Torturous thoughts of being the last man standing, the apocalypse, and the earth a burned out cinder raced through his mind. The desire to drink became imperative, the only solution to a problem so massive no single person could solve, anyway.

A drink will make life manageable.

He stood, opened up the top cabinet, and his shaking hand clutched the bottle of Tullamore Dew. He unscrewed the cap, and inhaled hints of sweet buttery caramel.

"Think about what you're doing, Kevin."

Corin's sensible voice echoed through his mind. The voice of practicality was always there to chastise, judge, and torment him. To hell with her nagging. He'd have a damn drink if he wanted.

He tilted his head back and gulped the whiskey straight from the bottle. Drops of sunshine spilled on his two-day-old beard and down the front of his shirt. The whiskey was warm, like heaven on a sunny day. He drank until his trembling muscles settled, his mind eased, and the pain subsided.

The screams outside grew faint as he staggered up the stairs. The boards over his windows shook and loosened, but he didn't care; he was on the whiskey highway to heaven.

He lumbered to his bedroom, wincing and

groaning with every step, closed the door, and hugged the bottle as he dropped to the closet floor.

With every sip of whiskey, he hated himself for falling off the wagon, but damned he needed this respite after what he had been through. He'd quit drinking tomorrow. Tonight, he didn't want to feel anything, just settle into Dew's loving embrace until he finally passed out.

There were no more screams, howls, or threats, just blackness.

Chapter Thirteen

Kevin awoke in the afternoon with a surge of hot bile racing up his throat. His hand clapped over his mouth, he staggered to his feet, and on legs like stilts, ran to the bathroom. With his hands gripping the sides of the toilet bowl, he vomited. Every time he inhaled, his stomach protested and sent up more liquor-tainted bile. The reek of puke was powerful in his nostrils, and the gunky pungency of the vomit lingered in his mouth. He tipped over on the floor, curled into a fetal position, and clasped his hands over his head. Drinking was hard work.

"I hope you're happy now."

It was Corin's voice and her deprecating tone that insisted she was always right, and he was always wrong. Head spinning, he found his feet, and wobbling to the medicine cabinet, he grabbed a bottle of aspirin and knocked four pills into his palm. Beyond the curtains in his bathroom window, daylight filtered in. He checked his cell phone. The battery was dead so he tossed it on the bed covers.

As he tottered out of his bedroom and down the stairs, he found that the fortifications had held. However, the mutants had loosened a few boards on the patio door, so there was work to be done.

He opened the knapsack he'd left on the counter and grabbed a bottle of water. After downing the aspirin, he ventured outside. The best thing about today was a sunny, clear sky. The warm sun reminded him of the fun summer things to do here at Mystic Estates: the pool, a tennis court, and a playground for the kids. Now, everything had changed. He needed to stay focused on survival, finding supplies, and locating Dr. Salkland.

He rubbed his burning eyes. The temptation to sleep off his hangover was great, but he had work to do on his reinforcements. The mutants would be back after sunset. He re-nailed the loose boards on the patio door and over the broken kitchen window. Satisfied, he dropped the hammer on the counter next to the baseball bat. Thanks to his hangover, he was bushed and sweaty. Why did he always overdo his drinking? Why was one drink never enough? He always drank until he got sloppy drunk. Corin was right. He had a drinking problem he couldn't fix on his own. He needed help: AA, detox, incarceration...the problem was overwhelming. How long could he go on like this? And then there was Frank and his mob of assassins. Kevin was in no shape to fight them off another night.

A thought popped into his head. *Where is Frank hiding?* He was always the first mutant on the scene, so that meant he was somewhere close-by.

With his stomach settled and the aspirin kicking in, he ate the peanuts he'd pilfered from the drugstore and drank more water. He packed the serrated knife and flashlight in his knapsack and, bat in hand, ventured out to find Frank's hiding place. He knew mutants could hide in tight spaces, like the narrow employee lockers, so he'd sweep the neighboring townhouses' nooks and crannies.

He started with Marge Thompson's place next door. She and Frank had a thing for each other, so maybe he was hiding there with her. The townhome layouts were pretty much the same as his, so it should be easy to find tight hiding places.

He entered Marge's place through the unlocked front door and opened up all the living room shades. Sunlight beamed in. She'd decorated the interior in Southwestern style: desert paintings, cactus knickknacks, Kokopelli Indian art, a setting far from the big-city realm. Bat at the ready and his nerves on full alert, he ventured into the kitchen. Lined up on the counter were rows of vodka bottles, some empty, most full, and candles, some new, some burned, and a box of stick matches, a shrine to her drinking problem. A picture of Frank Sinatra hung on the wall in her dining room. He opened the blinds over her patio door, and daylight illuminated her polished chrome appliances. The staircase toward the bedrooms lay in dark shadow, so he shucked off the knapsack, set it on the stove between the gas burners, and fished out the flashlight.

Having found no sign of Marge upstairs, he descended into her basement. Each step on the wooden stairs sounded like a groan. Beyond the flashlight beam, the cellar was dark as a dungeon.

He stalked farther into the basement, through a dusty laundry room, past the furnace, water heater, and into a storage room. Icy fingers crawled up his neck.

Something clicked behind him. He whirled with a gasp, but nothing was there. "Geeze." He had to get a grip on his nerves.

The room was as cluttered as most storage rooms. He shined the flashlight on two white wooden doors, a storage closet, and inside it he saw bottles of detergent, bleach, shampoos, a box of garbage bags, and other junk on six tiers of shelves. A pale bare foot stuck out from the top shelf.

He staggered back in surprise, and neck hairs prickling, he opened the doors wider, and shined the light on Marge, dressed in a pink nightgown. She'd crammed herself in tight.

"Nice try, Marge. I found you." He jammed the flashlight into his back pocket, reached up, grabbed her cold foot, and dragged her off the shelf.

She slammed to the floor, flat on her back, and

screamed.

He held the bat up high. "Where's your new boyfriend, Frank?"

"Leave me alone," she shrieked, waving the double-boned stub of her arm at him.

"I don't want to hurt you, Marge. Just tell me where I can find Frank. I'll leave you to go back to your nap."

"Go to hell." With incredible speed, she rolled over and crawled back to the storage closet.

As she climbed to the top shelf, fast as a lizard up a rock, he grabbed her leg and pulled her back down to the floor, kicking and screaming. "Marge. Stop it."

She hissed at him, spraying spittle. The Rage virus had destroyed this once beautiful and lonely woman.

He grabbed her flailing leg. "I want to help you."

"You can't help me, Kevin. Go back to your wife and kid."

"I'm going to find Dr. Salkland, talk to him about getting some trial samples of a serum for Corin and Ethan. I can get some for you too."

"I don't want no stinking serum. Get out of my house." She kicked at him, slipped out of his grasp, and scrambled off into the darkness.

He whirled as he removed the flashlight from his pocket then swept the beam around the cellar. "Marge, don't make me hunt you down."

"What are you going to do, Kevin, kill me?" Marge echoed back. "You didn't have the nerve to kiss me. I had to throw myself on you. I should kill you for that humiliation."

He stalked toward the sound of her voice. "I'm sorry, Marge. I was having a bad night."

"Wait until tonight. You haven't seen nothing yet. Frank is going to kill you."

A shadow darted to his left. He swung the flashlight in that direction. Marge slammed into him with fantastic speed and knocked him down. Pain shot through his shoulder, and the room whirled as the flashlight rolled against the far wall.

Suddenly, he felt her weight on his chest and foul fiery breath on his cheek. "Marge, don't do this."

"I could kill you right now, so easy, so

tempting, but you're Frank's fodder for tonight." She licked Kevin's face with a slimy tongue, and then she was gone.

For a moment in the darkness, silence pervaded like the vacuum of space. He rose to a crouch, his gaze darting across the room to where the flashlight lay, its beam a crescent on the wall.

"Come on, Marge. Don't let Frank call the shots. He's a terrible boss. Just tell me where he's hiding."

Silence. No footsteps. No heavy breathing.

"Marge. Talk to me. How about I get you a bottle of vodka from upstairs. We can keep things between us social, like it used to be."

"Pretty soon..." her voice came from the darkness, "the sun will go down, and then you'll be in deep shit. I suggest you run like a scared little girl, or Frank's going to finish you off."

He had to get through to her somehow. "I always took you for an independent woman, Marge. Why now do you let Frank fight your battles?"

"How dare you insult me?" she screeched as two glowing eyes surged at him.

He dropped the flashlight and grabbed her by the throat, stopping her at arm's length before she could sink her teeth into him. The light on the floor shined enough to reveal pure hatred on her face. Unabated rage, the animal in her was completely in control. He brandished the bat. "Don't make me use this on you."

Marge lashed out with clawed fingers. "I'm not afraid of you." Her fingernails were slashing close to his face. "Frank's gonna be shit out of luck when he finds out I've killed you myself."

Kevin had a way with women; he really knew how to piss them off. In this case, he'd escalated the danger he was in, as one scratch from her could infect him. He'd be a goner like everyone else. "Marge. I'm warning you."

She hissed and swiped.

He shoved her backwards and swung the bat. The crack of Mattingly against her skull didn't give him any satisfaction, and as she hit the floor, he wished he could've taken it back, not just the swing, but the insult that had set her off, as well. He had little time to dwell on his regrets, as her spastic tremors suddenly stilled, and she sat up.

The dropped flashlight revealed the loathing in her black-socketed eyeballs. He let Mattingly fly again, this time delivering a downward blow, much like an axe to firewood, caving in her skull and splattering blood and grey matter off into the darkness beyond the flashlight.

She slumped over and emitted a tiny squeak.

He picked up the flashlight, knowing this wasn't the end of Marge, as Mattingly hadn't put an end to the mutant in the employee locker, either. As Dr. Salkland had said, fire was the remedy. Marge would be back soon enough, mangled head and stubby-armed, testaments to the attacks he had rendered against her. On a normal day, he'd go to jail for his crimes, assault with a deadly weapon, attempted murder, but today was far from normal, as would be tomorrow and however many more days to come before Dr. Salkland found a cure.

He shouldered the bloody bat and pounded up the stairs to a townhouse filled with daylight. Frank had to be up here somewhere. Kevin had to give Marge credit for being loyal to Frank and keeping his location to herself. Now he'd have to tear this place apart to find him.

However, he didn't have much time. The sun shined brightly through the windows because it was low on the horizon. Within minutes, it would set, and Frank would come out of hiding and find him. If Marge was right, tonight would be a fight to the death, his unfortunately.

He entered the kitchen and let out a breath. At the counter, he used paper towels to wipe Marge's blood off the bat, then he moved to the cupboards and checked all the cabinets and shelves. The pantry. The coat closet. No Frank anywhere. "Damn it." Kevin had to get out of there. He rushed to the stove, and as he reached to put the flashlight in the knapsack, it quivered. That stopped him. He stared at the knapsack, thinking it might have been his imagination, but it quivered again.

"No way." He knelt to the window in the stove and shined the flashlight through the tinted glass. "Son of a bitch." Frank was folded up inside like some kind of circus contortionist.

"Gotcha."

He stood to examine the controls. *Gas...oven...*

He pushed the oven button. *I need full blast...* A digital panel was black. "Damn." With the power out, there was no way to open the gas valve, spark the igniter, or set the temperature. Frank was as safe in there as in a shoebox.

I need something to set him on fire.

One glance around the kitchen produced the answer. Vodka. Vodka was flammable. He rushed to Marge's vodka and candle shrine, grabbed a bottle, and read the label. *Smirnoff Blue: 100 proof, 50% alcohol.*

"Perfect." He grabbed the box of stick matches and opened the oven door. "Good morning, Frank."

"Get out of here, Tippler." His voice was weak and raspy, probably because his lungs were compressed so tightly, being crammed in such a confined space.

"How about a drink, Frank?" He uncapped the bottle and gave him a good soaking.

"What are you doing, Tippler?"

"It's a surprise."

Vodka dripped from Frank's clothes and pooled in the bottom of the oven. The fumes were intense, even for Kevin, the hard-core alcoholic he was. The bottle emptied, and he tossed it aside.

"Tippler?" Now there was panic in Frank's voice.

Kevin struck a stick match.

"You can't kill me, Tippler. I know where your family is holed up."

"Bullshit, Frank."

"Spare me, and I'll tell you where they are."

"You can't be trusted. You're stalling, buying time until the sun goes down. Then you'll become more powerful and a bigger asshole than your everyday normal self."

The match was burned halfway down the stick, the flame weakening by the second.

"I'm telling the truth, Tippler. It's about time you wised up."

Shadows lengthened as the sun lowered to the horizon.

"If I die, you'll never see them again."

What if he's right?

"Okay. Tell me where they are, and I'll blow out this match."

"Blow it out first."

"I've got a whole box of matches, Frank. You better talk fast."

The sun set, erasing all the shadows.

"Too late, Tippler. Now you'll never know." Frank stuck a leg out and started to unfold himself.

"Go to hell, Frank." Kevin tossed the withering match into the oven. With a whoosh, blue flame engulfed Frank. And just as quickly, he started screaming. His free pant-leg ignited, and his pale face was turning black. He tried to push out of the oven, but Kevin kicked him back in. The kitchen filled with the stink of singed hair and burning flesh. "I hope you burn in hell forever."

"Frank," Marge shouted as she charged into the kitchen.

Kevin stepped back to the counter and watched her kneel at the oven door and start pulling Frank out with her only hand. He'd already stopped screaming. The fire was an intense blue inferno, but it wouldn't last but a few seconds longer, so Kevin grabbed another vodka bottle, spun off the cap, and poured it on Marge's caved-in skullcap. She became an instant human torch, screaming as she stood, her pink nightgown ablaze and her raven hair a nest of fire and black smoke. "Kevin. What have you done?"

"You should've stayed downstairs."

She dropped to her knees, fell flat on her face, and burned.

The stench was awful, the smoke intolerable, but Kevin stood watch to be sure the place didn't catch fire and burn to the ground, taking his place with it.

Satisfied the duo was no longer a threat, he gathered his singed knapsack, retreated to his townhouse, and locked the door. In the aftermath, he felt sad, perhaps a bit depressed over losing two more people in his life. Good or bad, they'd both influenced him in some way, made him grow from adversity, and now they were gone. For Marge, he felt a great regret, but Frank, not so much. However, on the positive side, he'd released them from the torment their torturous lives had become.

He felt a sudden urge to be close to Ethan, in the shrine of his bedroom, where race cars were beds and hippos were best friends. He took

Mattingly upstairs with him, entered Ethan's room, and kneeled at his bed. His eyes welled with tears. Grasping the hippopotamus, he brought the little guy to his chest and wept for the loss of all that was good in his life, everything he'd destroyed, and even for the hippo who'd lost his best friend, Ethan.

We never got the chance to say goodbye to you, Ethan. We love you, buddy.

Howls and screams reverberated outside, and the mutants pounded on the doors and windows. He stood and looked down out the bedroom window in time to see Corin approach the front door, key in hand. The mutants parted and she let herself in, then they funneled in after her. He readied himself for another battle and gripped the bat.

Footsteps raced through the house and pounded up the stairs, then stopped at the doorway to Ethan's room.

Cold fear coursed through his veins at the thought of mutants ripping him to shreds, but five feet away stood Ethan.

Kevin's jaw dropped. The virus had done a

number on him. Black decay encircled his eyes, and pale skin flaked from his pallid face. His malevolent grin displayed rows of pointy teeth, and clawed fingers hung at his side, a signal for the others to hold fast. Any notion of hugging his son was sidelined with uncertainty about his intentions. "Son?" Kevin lowered the bat.

"Hi, Dad." Ethan stepped closer.

Kevin's lower lip trembled. "I've missed you, buddy."

"You still have time to become one of us. We can be a family again."

"But I don't want to be a mutant."

"Don't say that, Dad. The mutants behind me want to kill you."

"Hasn't there been enough killing?" What else could he say to the monster masquerading as his son? The son he would lose forever if the experimental serum didn't work. Kevin had to live long enough to find Dr. Salkland. There was no way Mattingly could get him out of this jam. There were too many mutants clustered behind Ethan, lusting for blood. Though Salkland had said mutants could not be reasoned with, Kevin had to try talking his way out of this room. "Ethan, I'm sorry I was selfish. If I had stopped drinking, your mom and I wouldn't have separated. We'd still be a family, most likely fighting this plague together."

"It doesn't matter now."

Heat rose in the back of his throat. "You're right...I just need a little time before you change me into a mutant."

"It won't make a difference."

"Maybe you're right, son, but then again, it might make all the difference in the world." He was thinking of Dr. Salkland's serum and how it could save his family and all of mankind.

Shuffling came from the hallway as the mutants made way for Corin. She entered the room and stood next to Ethan. Her hair was a rat-nest and her face a mask of the macabre. "What's it going to be, Kevin?"

"You have to give me more time, Corin."

"Time doesn't matter anymore."

Ethan touched Kevin's hand, the one holding the bat, as if he had no fear of Mattingly's brutal force. "Join us, Dad. You'll live forever."

Kevin furrowed his brow at the thought of immortality. Did he want to be a flesh-eater forever? What would happen when the last human on earth had been devoured? Would the mutants start feeding on each other? Until then, he wouldn't have to run anymore, in fear of the mutants, but that concession would be akin to selling his soul to the devil himself. He wanted no part of living in a true hell on earth. "Son, please understand. Living forever isn't the point. It's how we live that matters."

Corin raked the air with her clawed fingers. "Typical Kevin. Always making the wrong decision."

"It's painless, Dad. Don't make us kill you."

Kevin raised the bat. "I won't go easy."

The mutants pressed through the doorway, their black eyes enraged and teeth chattering.

His next move was to swing the bat at Ethan's head, bash in his skull like he'd done the others, then recoil and smash Corin's face to pulverized bone. However, some internal force stronger than the pull of alcohol made it impossible for him to strike a violent blow against his family. Instead, he turned to the window behind him and set Mattingly to the task of busting out the glass. It was a fifteen-foot drop to the bushes below, which broke his fall, and he rolled out of the leafy scrub to the lawn, bat at the ready, expecting an immediate battle, but it appeared all the mutants had gone inside the townhouse.

The lawn was bathed in moonlight, and the street was bathed in blood. Mutants down the block lumbered through the carnage of wrecked cars and strewn bodies, and mutants appeared on the rooftops across the street. Behind him, mutants dropped from the broken window where Corin looked out and shouted, "Kill him."

As he assessed which way to run, a thick mist crept along the ground. With cold dread squeezing his chest, he sprinted toward Mystic Estates' front gate. Mutants came out of the woodwork and joined the mob on his tail. He ran past the covered pool toward the clubhouse. Candlelight flickered through gaps in the boarded-up windows, and some kind of vegetation hung from the front doorframe. Perhaps other survivors were holed up inside.

After Sunset

Just as that thought crossed his mind, the front door opened, and a familiar redheaded woman waved him to run toward her. There were no black rings around her eyes, so he knew she wasn't trying to trap him. She was a survivor, like himself. As soon as he changed directions, a mutant behind him shouted, "Stop him."

Mutant footfalls thundered a few yards behind him. He dove through the entrance, and the woman slammed shut the door behind him. Screams and howls echoed through the night. He crashed into a wall and crumpled to the floor. A crowd of people armed with clubs, bats, and knives surrounded him.

"Drop your weapon, scumbag." A bearded brute brandished a machete big enough to behead an elephant.

Kevin set down the bat and raised his hands. "I'm not a mutant."

"He's the guy I told you about," the redhead said. "Stayed alive out there all this time."

"How do we know he ain't been bit?"

"Were you bitten?" the woman who let him in asked.

"No. I'm fine."

She helped him to his feet. "You're safe here."

"I can't believe it. I thought I was the last man standing." He observed the faces around him. There were five men, three women, and two children. Behind the survivors stood a pool table, television, couch, and chairs.

This clubhouse could be the last safe place on earth.

"I'm Janet," the woman said. "Rambo here is Thomas." She indicated the burly man wearing glasses, the guy with the big knife.

"I'm Kevin. Kevin Tippler."

Janet looked him up and down. "You must be starving."

Thomas groaned. "We can't feed any more people."

"We can't just throw him out."

"Prove he's not one of them." He took a wreath down from the wall and handed it to her.

"Okay. If that'll make you happy." She gave the wreath to Kevin. "Put this around your neck."

It smelled nice but: "What is it?"

"Sage. If you're infected, you'll start foaming at the mouth and go into convulsions before you pass out."

"That's totally unnecessary. I told you I was fine."

"Do it," Thomas said.

The others pointed their weapons at Kevin.

Thomas snarled. "If he tries anything, guys, don't hesitate to kill him."

"Okay, take it easy," Janet said to the others.

Kevin put the wreath on and glared at those who didn't trust him. "See? I'm still standing."

All the survivors lowered their weapons, and Janet shook Kevin's hand. "Congratulations. Now how about something to eat?"

Thomas shouldered his machete. "No offense, but we gotta be careful with our rations."

Janet stabbed a finger at him. "What do you want to do, let him starve? There's not many of us left."

Thomas grumped. "When we run out of food, we'll have to make some hard choices."

"Choices?"

"Like who are we going to eat first."

She scoffed. "Don't worry, Thomas. Nobody's going to eat you. You're rotten to the core."

The others laughed.

"Fine." Thomas stormed to the stairs that led to the basement. "Don't mind him," Janet said. "He hates everybody."

"I get it. I'm a liability, but I'm just happy to see real people." He removed the wreath from his neck and hung it back up on the wall. "How did you know sage was lethal to mutants?"

"Not lethal, just debilitating. We experimented with different herbs and spices, garlic for starters, but the mutants kept pounding on our door until we tried sage. That's kept them at bay, but sage dries out. We need to find fresh supplies, which has become very difficult. One day, the fresh sage will be unavailable, and they'll be back to break through our defenses."

"Thanks for your help, Janet. I'd like to return the favor."

"How?"

"I'm going to find Dr. Salkland in Yonkers. He's developed a serum against the Rage virus, but it's in limbo while the FDA awaits test results that can take months. If he gives me a few of his experimental vials, I'll bring some to you."

She scoffed. "Easier said than done, Kevin. What makes you think you'll live long enough to get to Yonkers, and why would the doctor give you any of his serum?"

"I've got to try, and I've got to ask. My wife and son's lives are at stake, so I'm highly motivated."

The mutants milled about on the curb, their screams as loud as a bloodcurdling choir from hell.

"Jesus," Janet said. "They're really in a frenzy out there. What's got them so worked up?"

"It's me they want."

"Why?"

"Remember I told you about my wife and son?"

She frowned.

"They're leading the pack. I wouldn't join them, so they want me dead."

"And you'll risk your life to save them? That makes no sense. They're the enemy now, there's no changing that."

"If I get the serum, there's a chance, no matter how small, that I can cure them and put our family back together."

"I see. You're a strange bird, Mr. Tippler."

Thomas pounded up the stairs. "What is everybody doing up here? Get downstairs. You're agitating the mutants."

Their screams increased to a crescendo. Then they chanted, "Give us Tippler. Give us Tippler."

Thomas grabbed Kevin's arm and shook him. "You brought this trouble with you. I knew we shouldn't have let you in."

Adrenaline poured into Kevin's veins, and he shoved Thomas back. "Keep your hands off me."

"He's going to get us all killed."

Janet pressed between them. "Give him a chance. He's been through hell, besides, he has a plan to save us, which is more than I can say for you."

Thomas stood over Janet and leaned toward Kevin, glaring at him with sheer malice in his eyes. "We're not losing this sanctuary. We worked hard for it. If those mutants get in here, I'll kill you first, Tippler."

"Back off, Thomas," Janet said.

With nowhere to turn, Kevin stood his ground.

After Sunset

The mutants want to kill me. Now the humans threaten to kill. A guy can't get a break in this world.

"We'll figure this out tomorrow," Janet said. "When the sun comes up. Now let's go downstairs and eat."

"Dad, can you come outside? We won't hurt you."

Kevin froze, drawn to his son's voice, though he knew his words were a lie. An image of playing baseball with Ethan crept into his mind. *Watch me hit a home run, Dad. I'm going to play for the Yankees someday.* It was a world long gone, but a world Kevin wanted restored so badly he'd risk death on the road to Yonkers.

"Is that your son?" Janet asked.

Kevin slumped. Waves of sadness overwhelmed him. It would have been better if Ethan had died, and in a way, he did die; the boy he once knew was gone, but the love he held for his son lived on, now as it would forever.

"He was my son."

"I'm sorry for your loss."

"Kevin?" another familiar voice shouted from the mob. "Your son wants to see you. Be a real dad, for once. Come out."

Janet gasped. "Who's that?"

"My wife."

"Sounds like you guys have issues beyond this pandemic."

"We will not leave until you come out," Corin shouted. "Tell your new friends inside. They're all going to die."

Thomas growled out, "I told you... he's a clear and present danger."

"Shut up, Thomas."

Kevin looked at Janet. "I can't stay."

"I know." She took his arm. "The sun will be up soon enough. Let's eat."

Chapter Fourteen

The next morning, Janet packed bottled water and some canned goods into a knapsack, and threw in a flashlight. "I hope this will be enough. Good luck finding Dr. Salkland."

"Do you have a working cell phone?"

"They're all dead. We doubt Vericom is operational. Who do you want to call?"

"I'd like to Google Dr. Salkland, or check Yelp for an address and phone number."

"There's no Wi-Fi, anyway. No power."

"Then I'll have to check with hospitals, Urgent Care centers, and medical facilities along the way to see if anyone knows the address of his lab in Yonkers. You guys stay safe while I'm gone."

"We're going out to scavenge for supplies and fresh sage."

Thomas stormed up to Kevin. "Good thing you're leaving."

Kevin scowled at him. "I knew a guy once. Frank Cicero. He was a prick just like you, and you know what? He's dead, so being a prick didn't help him survive, just made everyone around him miserable and on edge. So tell me, Thomas, do you really want to be like Frank?"

"I'm protecting my interests." Thomas pulled a gun from his waistband and pointed it at the ceiling. "Don't come back here, or you'll be looking down the barrel of this gun."

"What's wrong with you, Thomas?" Janet asked. "He's going out there to help us."

Thomas stuck the gun back in his pants. "The Lord helps those who help themselves. If you think he's going to come back some kind of hero, think again. Heroes are the first to die."

Kevin ticked his tongue. "I think you're one sick puppy."

Thomas sneered. "I don't care what you think."

Janet took Kevin's hand. "Safe travels."

"Thanks for everything." He walked out the clubhouse, and the door locked behind him.

Chapter Fifteen

O n this cloudless day, Kevin returned home to see what the mutants had left of his belongings. As he reached his house, his mouth dropped open. The mutants destroyed his home, smashed the windows, upturned the table and chairs, and tore apart his sofa. Upholstery stuffing from the cushions was scattered all over the living room floor. Written in blood on the walls, a warning:

WE'RE GOING TO FIND YOU

Worse, they'd smashed his liquor bottles, probably Corin's doing. He wiped sweat from his brow. All his hard work had been destroyed in one night, and he doubted he could fix anything before sundown.

Adrenaline boiled in his veins, and he slammed the bat against the bloody wall. *I have to find a new place to hide out, and fast.* He hurried to the garage, hoping he could ride away on his bike, but the mutants had slashed the tires and bent the frame.

You're going to pay for this...all of you.

However, hunting them down was going to take time, and what was the use, anyway? He had seen the mutants' numbers. Their ranks were growing because the virus had no cure. Dr. Salkland was the world's only hope.

He ventured out on foot, searching for a better mode of transportation. After a short trek to Corin's parents' townhome to get his car, he found it had been totaled right where it was parked. The mutants had used it for a trampoline, dented the roof and hood and fenders, busted out all the glass, and slashed all the tires. He wanted to be pissed off, but what good would it do?

A ways down the road, near the front gate, he found an old mountain bike in a garage. It was serviceable, and he rode out of Mystic Estates.

He pedaled south on Albany Post Road, weaving around wrecked and abandoned cars and startling murders of crows that picked at the dead bodies lying about. At times, the stench became overpowering, but he pedaled on, past looted and burnt stores all the way into Ossining.

There he found a motorcycle shop, Kawasaki and Ducati, with the windows broken out and dirt bikes strewn about, tipped and smashed. He parked the mountain bike and stalked into the building where he found shelves of parts and riding gear knocked over and scattered. In the back, on its kickstand, there stood a knobby-tired rally bike, complete with racing stripes and checkered flags and a key in the ignition. He hopped on, fired up the noisy engine, and steered it out to the front of the shop. With a half a day of sunlight left and a half tank of gas, he'd easily make it to Yonkers and back before dark.

He nabbed a helmet off a 4-wheeler lying on its side, strapped into it, and raced onto the highway. The off-road machine made easy work of dodging debris, cutting through parking lots and front lawns as he knitted his way southward. Occasionally he'd cross paths with uninfected people walking the streets in shock, slowly and stiff as zombies.

During his fervent search, he stopped at a Doctor's office; no one was there, then headed south, and stopped at an urgent care clinic where the small staff had set up a triage unit for victims of the Rage virus. The mutants were housed in dog-kennel cages where they attacked the chain-link to get at anyone who came close. An attendant explained, "Once the FDA approves Dr. Salkland's serum, he'll send us some vials, and we'll try it on these mutants to see if it works. If anyone can cure this plague, he can."

"Do you know where his lab is located?"

"The Global Medical Building in Yonkers, but you can't get in there. It's a highly restricted lab."

"Thanks for the warning." Kevin jumped on the bike and tore off south on Broadway.

It took him twenty minutes to knock out the twelve-mile ride to Global Medical. He jumped off the bike in front of the building. The place was an apocalyptic scene of upturned cars, smoldering fires, and smashed windows. It appeared the hospital staff had barricaded the front doors with office furniture, chairs and couches, but the mutants had blown right through them. A massive diesel generator lugged and sputtered, and as he entered the front lobby, the ceiling lights flickered to the same rhythm.

He stepped over bodies, some with their throats ripped out and others half eaten. The nauseating stench of death slapped him in the face. Black flies buzzed around the corpses, and white maggots wriggled in the rotting meat. Blood was smeared across the walls. It must've been one hell of a battle, but the victors were obviously not these poor souls.

He followed the signs toward the immunology department. Along the way, there were no survivors to find. An arrow pointed down a flight of stairs to immunology, and as much as his better sense told him not to go down there, he continued on his quest into the bowels of Global Medical. Despite the fact it was still daylight, he pulled Mattingly from his backpack, just in case he ran into a rogue mutant or overzealous orderly.

More blood and stench greeted him in the stairwell. At the bottom, each footstep echoed down a long hallway, the ceiling lights on the verge of failing.

The heavy feeling of terror in his chest accelerated to dizzying panic, but his resolve had not dwindled in the least. His skin squirmed with the fear that black-rimmed eyes were watching him from the shadows, but he pressed on...for Corin, for Ethan, and for the others barricaded in the clubhouse.

When he reached the door to immunology, he found it wide open, and his better judgment told him not to go any farther.

"Dr. Salkland," he shouted into the room. "Are you in here?"

No answer.

The miracle man he was looking for was probably dead.

"Dr. Salkland, please."

If he was dead, there'd be no information here, no hope, but the attendant had said the vials of serum were here, waiting to be sent...

"Dr. Salkland. I'm coming in." He stalked inside, and as he stepped over yet another dead body, the ceiling lights went out then flashed back on. That generator was on the brink of a major shutdown.

Following the signs to the lab, he crept down another corridor, bat at the ready and terror like a heavy boot on his chest. Each time he thought to turn and run, Corin and Ethan flashed in his mind, so he stayed on course for their sakes.

When he reached Doctor James Salkland's lab, the ceiling lights went out. Blackness engulfed him; he couldn't see his hand in front of his face. Working by feel alone, he pulled the flashlight from his backpack, clicked it on, and took a deep, calming breath as bright light reclaimed the room.

He swept the beam across counters and chairs overturned, and three stainless-steel examination tables, each with a corpse lying on it, all three in various stages of dissection. On the far wall, there was a long counter and a man in a white coat hunched before a microscope.

"Dr. Salkland? Is that you?"

The man didn't answer. He didn't move.

Kevin stalked up behind him and touched his shoulder.

No response.

He pulled back on the doctor's shoulder and heard a slurping sound. The mutants had shoved his head into the eyepieces, crushing his eyeballs. Salkland stared out empty black sockets, a haunting sight in the flashlight beam. A name badge on his lab coat confirmed it was him. The hope of the world was now dead and gone. An anvil dropping on Kevin's head would have been less of a shock. Curiously, a piece of paper protruded from the top pocket of Salkland's lab coat. Kevin pulled it out and unfolded it. Under the flashlight beam it read:

If you are reading this, I must be dead. Please don't let my research go to waste. In my pants pocket are the keys to the high cabinet above the microscope. There you'll find a stash of vials containing the serum I've developed. It's raw and untested, but it's lethal to the Rage virus, both as a vaccine and a cure, but its efficacy in humans hasn't been proven. Take the vials to the nearest military facility. They'll know what to do with the serum. Good luck. Respectfully, Doctor James Salkland.

Kevin fished a ring of keys out of the doctor's pocket then flashed the light up to a glass cabinet in which he could see vials of serum. It was a wonder the mutants hadn't destroyed them after killing the doctor.

He examined the keys, determined some were

for doors, one was for a Mercedes, and several were smaller, and these he tested before one finally opened the cabinet. "Bingo."

He snatched up two fistfuls of vials and several syringes, then stuffed them in his backpack. Ready to retreat, he stopped to pat the doctor's shoulder. "Thanks, Doc. You may not have saved the world, but with any luck, you've saved my family."

With the flashlight beam leading the way, he ran back into the hallway and swung the light to the left and right. A white face reflected back from the darkness, its black-rimmed eyes glaring at him from twenty steps away. Its head skimmed the ceiling as the giant mutant grunted and lumbered toward him with its clawed hands extended.

He ran to the left and jumped over corpses. One grabbed his leg. He gasped, whacked the corpse with his bat, yanked free, and raced up the stairs. When he reached the lobby floor, he realized he was in big trouble. The sun was going down, and worse, the bodies that were lying on the floor were gone. A quick glance around revealed white faces glaring at him from the shadows, captives there until the last rays of sunlight defused into twilight. He didn't have much time.

He ran out the entrance to discover his motorbike was gone.

What else can go wrong?

Maybe the doc's car was around here somewhere. He took out the doctor's key ring and found the one with a Mercedes symbol on the thumb pad. Two screaming mutants raced toward him. He depressed the panic button on the key-fob. The car's alarm chirped, and flashing lights gave away its location, maybe fifty feet away and sandwiched between wrecked cars. The mutants were almost on him. He swung the bat, knocking one over, but the other grabbed hold of the bat. Kevin kicked him in the groin, and he let go just as a raging horde exploded from the hospital and charged toward him.

His brain went into flight mode. He rushed to the car and unlocked the door with the remote. By now, the mutants were only fifteen feet away. He shucked off the backpack, threw it and the bat onto the passenger seat, and jumped in behind the wheel, but as he pulled the door closed, a pale arm wedged itself inside, and a clawed hand pawed at his face. He kicked the door open, shoving the mutant backwards. It slammed into its followers, bowling them over, giving Kevin the second he needed to close and lock the door.

As he started the engine, the enraged mutants surrounded the car and started banging on the windows. He gunned the gas and ploughed through the throng as the heavy-framed Mercedes shoved wrecked vehicles out of his path. Tires skidded and thumped over bodies as the car raced through the parking lot, even as some mutants hung on. To his right, the giant mutant he'd dodged in the basement charged from the hospital's entrance, knocking over other mutants as it gave chase.

Kevin glanced up at the rearview mirror and saw the giant mutant gaining on him. If the monster should manage to grab onto the rear bumper, he'd be a dead man.

Fighting panic, he wrestled the steering wheel left and right, dodging as many mutants as he could. They scattered in every direction. Already the hood was dented, and the windshield was cracked from all the collisions. Gritting his teeth, he cleared the hospital parking lot and careened the car onto Broadway, heading north.

His nerves were frayed to confetti as he steered a course toward Mystic Estates. Although he had survived with a potential cure, getting back to the clubhouse in one piece would be a death-defying challenge.

The clubhouse is the only safe place. With a cure in hand, Thomas will be less likely to shoot me.

However, getting past the hordes of mutants rampaging through the night had to come first. After sunset was their time to reign supreme, and he would not be welcome in their territories.

He gripped the wheel with an iron will, dodging overturned cars, burning rubble, and groping mutants. At times, the heavy Mercedes ploughed through piles of debris that blocked the road in this obstacle course from hell. Kevin noticed there were no planes in the sky, no trains on the tracks, and no boats and barges on the Hudson. Civilization had come to a screeching halt.

As he blew through the front gate of Mystic

Estates, screaming, ashen-faced mutants ran after him. There must have been hundreds more than before, as the Rage virus had spread exponentially since he'd left.

A mutant jumped into the road, blocked his path, and stared at him with an icy glare. He gunned the accelerator. The mutant thudded off the fender and rolled to the ground, but jumped right back up again and raged in pursuit.

As he neared the clubhouse, he hoped Thomas wouldn't shoot him as he tried to pass vials of serum to Janet. She might be able to immunize her fellow survivors and get the rest to the military. Maybe their scientists and doctors can put an end to the pandemic.

A gang of mutants stood in front of the clubhouse, but he didn't see Ethan or Corin. As he drove up, the monsters turned and stabbed their clawed fingers at him. He stopped, gunned the engine, and flashed the lights. The mutants held fast. During this standoff, he pulled a vial and syringe from the backpack, charged the syringe with serum, capped the needle, and slipped it into his right front pocket.

The mutants charged.

He ploughed the Mercedes into them and skidded to a stop at the front door. This would only buy him a few precious seconds, so he wasted no time bailing out of the car with Mattingly and the backpack. Three steps later, he was pounding on the clubhouse door. "Janet," he screamed. "Open the door."

A clawed hand grabbed his shoulder and spun him around. He swung Mattingly, and the blow knocked the mutant to the ground, but others were racing toward him, just seconds away. The car created an obstacle between him and the mob.

"What are you doing here, Kevin?" Janet shouted.

Thomas's voice followed. "We're not letting him in."

"I have a serum, a vaccine and a cure."

"Thomas, you hear that? I have to let him in."

The door opened, and Kevin shoved the backpack to Janet. "It's all in here."

Thomas greeted him with a gun barrel to his stomach. "I told you not to come back here."

The mutants were running around the car and

climbing over the roof. Their bloodcurdling howls made the hairs on the back of his neck stand up.

"Vaccinate yourselves and take the rest to the nearest military base. They'll know—"

Thomas fired the gun.

A hot bullet tore into Kevin's belly. He back-stepped as the pain buckled him over.

The clubhouse door slammed shut, and mutants grabbed him, and with grips of steel, they carried him to the street. "We finally have him." They dropped him on the pavement as if he were nothing but road-kill.

Blood gushed from his stomach and his head felt dizzy. His eyes fluttered and he smelled chocolate chip cookies fresh from the oven.

"Don't kill him," Ethan said.

Kevin wanted to tell his son that death was welcomed, in fact, because he had given Janet the potential cure, his death would not be in vain. With any luck, when the sun came up, she could find a military base and get it into the right hands. He had done what he had set out to do. The rest was up to the survivors.

By now, the mutants had surrounded him.

Ethan and Corin knelt at his side. Her eyes were crimson dots, and she shook his shoulder. "What did you give them?"

He managed a smile. It was nice to have gotten one over on Corin, but he had one more surprise for her. He surreptitiously slipped his right hand into his pocket, slid out the charged syringe, and flipped off the needle cap with his thumb.

"Tell me what you gave them."

"Better yet, let me show you."

"Watch out, Mom," Ethan shouted.

Kevin reached up, jabbed the needle into Corin's neck, and pushed down on the plunger.

The mutants stepped back in shock.

Corin had no immediate reaction. Then terror leaked from her eyes. She yanked the needle out of her neck and held it in front of Kevin's face. "What the hell is in this?"

"You'll see." Kevin coughed.

A few seconds passed and nothing happened. He figured the serum was a failure, but at least the history books would say he had died trying. Then her body started shaking, as if she were holding a two hundred amp power cable, until she collapsed to the ground.

"Mom." Ethan rushed to her side, his eyes wide. "What's wrong?"

Corin's crimson eyes changed to white, the black rings receded, and her pale skin returned to normal.

Kevin laughed and then hacked up blood.

It works. Mankind has a chance to survive.

"Dad. What did you do to Mom?"

Hot pain stormed through his insides. "I have some serum for you, too, son." But thanks to Thomas's bullet, Kevin would not live to see a brighter future for his family and the human race. His heartbeat slowed. He heard music, a choir singing... "Farewell, Ethan. I hope...I see you in heaven someday." His eyes rolled back, and Ethan's face faded to black.

"No," Ethan cried and sank his teeth into Kevin's shoulder.

There were no white lights and pearly gates. Only eternal nothingness, a place where nothing mattered, where he had no recollection that he'd ever lived, ever loved, ever existed, until, as a free-diver would shoot to the surface, consciousness returned; Kevin awoke with a gasp and opened his eyes.

The mutants didn't seem surprised when he stood and clenched his claw-like fists as he felt the power and strength surging through him like a current of electricity. His senses sharpened. From a mile away, he could hear a rabbit hopping through the grass, and below, the gishing of worms as they dug through the soil. The darkness of night was bright as day, but most of all, he noticed a fierce hunger burning inside, a lust for blood and red meat.

"You're one of us now, Dad," Ethan said with a grin.

Kevin looked at his clawed hands. "I can't believe how wonderful it feels."

"I told you so. You don't have to run anymore."

Corin stepped up next to him and looped her arm around his waist. "Welcome home, Kevin."

Her face was pale as death, and her eyes were ringed with decay. "But I thought you...I thought the serum cured you."

"I bit her too," Ethan said. "She'll be fine now."

Kevin thought about that, didn't take a second for him to realize the cure was only temporary. People could be re-infected as easily as they were the first time. It was worthless as a vaccine. The Rage virus had not been defeated, after all.

Corin hugged Ethan. "Thanks for saving me."

"You're welcome, Mom."

Kevin felt his teeth grow to points and expand in his mouth. The wound in his stomach had completely healed.

No more pain. No more running. No more thirst for alcohol. Just a thirst for human blood.

Ethan took Kevin's hand just like any dutiful son would do. "Will you help us kill Janet and the others, Dad?"

What good dad wouldn't help his son?

"Of course, buddy. I especially have a bone to pick with Thomas."

Kevin and his reunited family strode back to the clubhouse with hundreds of mutants screaming bloody murder behind them.

Jim Keane

Born in the Bronx, **Jim Keane** holds a Bachelor of Arts in English from Mount Saint Mary College and has completed many creative writing courses. He's written several short stories and three novels and has more tomes in the works. Jim resides in Westchester, New York, with his family.

Read More from Jim Keane

 **Astra's Revenge**

When a syndicate assassin kills the mother of a circus fortune teller, he can run but he can't hide from Astra's black magic and her crystal ball.

 **The Midnight Train Murders**

A disgraced journalist, hoping to regain his prestige, investigates the murder of passengers on the midnight train to Crotonville, a reporter's dream story that turns into a nightmare.

 **Gateway**

A tragic encounter with a bullet-riddled man in a dark alley catapults computer-nerd Sean Calhoun into a deadly cat and mouse race to protect a stolen cell phone that can connect to the dead.

www.twbpress.com/authorjimkeane.html

Jim Keane

**Enjoy more short stories and novels by
many talented authors at**

www.twbpress.com

**Science Fiction, Supernatural, Horror, Thrillers,
Romance, and more**